P9-CMT-621

By Michael de Guzman

THE BAMBOOZLERS

Michael de Guzman

THE BAMBOOZLERS

FARRAR STRAUS GIROUX ■ NEW YORK

www.fsgkidsbooks.com

Library of Congress Cataloging-in-Publication Data
De Guzman, Michael.
The bamboozlers / Michael de Guzman.— 1st ed.
p. cm.
Summary: Nothing exciting ever happens to twelve-year-old Albert Rosegarden
until he meets his grandfather for the first time and the pair travel to Seattle,
Washington, where Albert becomes a partner in his grandfather's elaborate
scheme to "con a con man."
ISBN-13: 978-0-374-30512-3
ISBN-10: 0-374-30512-9
1. Grandfathers—Fiction.   2. Swindlers and swindling—Fiction.   3. Seattle
(Wash.)—Fiction.   I. Title.

PZ7.D3655 Bam 2005
[Fic]—dc22

2004057670

To my grandson, Timothy,
and my grandfathers, Emilio and Chim

With thanks to W.A.

THE BAMBOOZLERS

HOME ON THE RANGE

Albert Rosegarden raced through downtown Mountain View, Idaho, on his bicycle like his tail was being snapped at by a fork of lightning. Albert Rosegarden was in an enormous hurry. He had to get home before his mother got the call. So he could explain his side of it first. His bicycle was painted silver by his own hand. It had only one gear, no fenders, bald tires, and no brakes. He'd just been suspended from school.

"I see we're picking up right where we left off last year," Mr. Grimes, the assistant principal, had said to him not more than five minutes ago. "You're back in school a week and already in trouble. I'm suspending you for three days. You should be proud of yourself, Mr. Rosegarden. Only twelve years old and on your way to becoming a career criminal."

Albert didn't buy into that idea for any part of a second. He was just calling them as he saw them. He wasn't guilty of anything worse than that. If Mrs. Hissendale hadn't said that the earth was round, like the ball she was bouncing on the floor, if she hadn't said it with that I-know-more-than-you-do expression on her face, he might not have said anything.

He pedaled furiously past Davis's General Store, which featured work clothes, then past Sylvia's Gourmet Shop, which was big on goat cheese, then past Owen's gas station, which offered free air. It was Thursday, the eighth of September. It was ninety-four degrees, and the wind was blowing dust in three directions at once. The day had been heading downhill ever since he'd opened his eyes and heard his mother in the kitchen.

Thursday was one of his mother's days off, the other being Sunday. Elly was a cocktail waitress at the Goat Herder Lounge, the only bar in Mountain View with a live piano player. The only mountain in Mountain View was so far away that its dim outline was barely visible on a clear day.

"I'm your mother," Elly announced every Thursday

morning of the school year. "I can get up once a week to have breakfast with you."

Being that this was the first Thursday of the school year, Elly had decided on pancakes. Elly didn't do well in the kitchen on five hours' sleep. She wasn't much for cooking under the best of circumstances. The batter was lumpy. The outsides of the pancakes were burned. The centers were squishy.

Albert had put the first two pancakes his mother served him into his pants pockets when he thought she wasn't looking, then declared himself full.

"Those were delicious," he'd said.

"Don't forget where you put them," she'd said, bringing her cup of coffee to the table. She never ate anything for breakfast. "They'll get sticky and you won't be able to get them out."

He'd put them back on his plate.

"I wish I was a better cook," she'd said.

He'd eaten the pancakes then, squishy centers and all. He tried as hard as he could, as often as he could, to please her. Especially when she started getting philosophical.

With the pancakes fermenting in his stomach, he'd ridden off to school. On the way, the Hansen brothers, Howard and Martin, ran him off the road with their pickup. It was something they did most mornings. It was their weak-minded notion of a joke. He'd gone barreling off the shoulder into a herd of grazing goats, who took off bleating like they'd been attacked by a pack of wolves.

He flew past Belcher's Insurance, which promised honest coverage for all, then past Simmons' Jewelers, which had a three-foot-high fake diamond ring hanging over its door, then past Crystal's Diner, which was famous for its pie.

Albert's pale blue eyes squinted like he was looking for something he couldn't quite see. His curly black hair fell over his forehead. He had the face of an angel, of a boy who could do no wrong. He was small for his age. And watchful.

A quarter of a mile outside town he turned up a dirt road that was marked by a weather-beaten mailbox and a cow in a ditch. Two hundred yards later he arrived at a mobile home that was secured to a concrete slab. Elly was sitting in the doorway. They'd rented it ever since she'd decided that they'd spent enough time on the road. That was two years ago.

"We're staying here," she'd said while they were consuming their first humongous wedges of Crystal's chocolate cream pie.

At the time it hadn't made any difference to Albert. It didn't seem to him then that one place was any better or worse than any other.

"I'm tired of driving," she'd said.

He watched her stand as he parked his bicycle next to her fourteen-year-old Ford, which was rusting out around the wheels. She was tall, with honey blond hair and deep green eyes. Albert thought she'd be elected Miss Mountain View in a landslide, if there were such a thing.

"I'll get a pail of water to stick my feet in," Elly said. "We'll sit out back and talk."

"It wasn't my fault," he said, following her into the trailer. The kitchen was the size of a boat's galley.

Elly put the pail in the sink and started filling it. "It's never your fault. Mr. Grimes thinks you're going to end up in jail."

"I'm not going to end up in jail," Albert said. "All that happened was that Mrs. Hissendale said the planet Earth was round like a ball."

"And you said?"

"That it was shaped more like her head."

"You told Mrs. Hissendale her head looked like the planet Earth?"

"Well, it's a lot closer to that than it is to a ball," he said. "It's like an egg. Or a pear."

"You can't tell your teacher her head looks like a planet," she said.

"Then she shouldn't tell us stuff that isn't true," he said.

"A lot of people will tell you things that aren't true," she said. "Sometimes they do it on purpose, sometimes they don't know any better. What matters is understanding the difference. And knowing when to speak up and when to stay quiet. It's tricky. But you have to learn."

"In first grade," Albert said, "when that teacher told me about George Washington chopping down the cherry tree and how he never told a lie, I told her she was wrong because you told me the story was made up."

"I also read you *King Arthur*," she said, "but you didn't go around knocking people off their horses."

"I didn't know anybody with a horse," he said.

They moved outside and sat in the two white plastic stacking chairs which were set next to the barbecue grill. Elly put her feet into the cold water and sighed.

"What am I going to do with you, Albert?"

"Take me out to the middle of the forest and leave me there," he said. He was hoping for a smile.

"There is no forest here," she said. "And even if there were, you'd just find your way back. You were suspended twice last year. You have to stop. You need an education or you'll end up busting your behind for tips when you're forty and living in a trailer."

"You're forty-two," Albert said.

"Don't be a wise guy. Nobody likes a wise guy. I was making a point. It was an example. You have to learn how to take care of yourself. You have to learn how to behave in school. You have to take other people into account. You have to grow up."

"It's hard to grow up."

Elly laughed. "Where'd you read that?"

"In a magazine at the dentist's office."

"It's not news. Of course it's hard to grow up. It's hard to be grown up. The whole thing is hard."

"How come you're not mad at me?"

"I am mad at you. I just don't have the energy to yell. I'm going to ask you to give me a break. I need a vacation."

"Go somewhere," Albert said. "I can take care of myself."

"Right here is as far away as I can afford to go," Elly said. "What I'm asking is for you to be a little smarter."

"Okay," Albert said.

Elly leaned back and closed her eyes.

Albert thought about what he could do to help his mother go on vacation. He added up what he could make from odd jobs every week, then added his entire allowance and concluded that it would take about a thousand years to save enough to make it happen.

He thought about what it would be like to leave Mountain View and go off on an adventure himself. There had to be more to life than what he'd encountered so far.

They picked up the conversation later, when Albert decided to help his mother make dinner.

"You could get a different job," he said. "You're too old to be standing all night." He was opening a can of baked beans.

"I'm not too old for anything," Elly said. She was shaping a dollar thirty-nine cents' worth of ground beef into two hamburgers.

"Why do you have to work at night?"

"Because that's when I can make the most money."

"Why can't we go someplace else?"

"Why would we do that? You want cheese?"

"I do," he said. "It would be different someplace else, that's all. Maybe even better."

Elly gave her son a long look. "From the time your father left us in Myrtle Beach, South Carolina, until the day we got here was seven years of hard living in a large part of the continental United States. I don't remember seeing anything better that would be available to people in our economic bracket."

"Different would be enough," he said.

"It would be the same for us, Albert. I wish that wasn't so, but there it is."

They put the pot of beans, the hamburgers, the cheese slices, buns, ketchup, and two glasses of iced tea on the banged-up old tray Elly had brought home from work, and went out back.

"Remember the time we drove across Arkansas all night?" Albert asked.

His mother placed the hamburgers on the grill.

He loved the way they sizzled when they first went on.

"We had a flat tire, ran out of gas, and a hose broke and all the water leaked out of the radiator," she said.

He was eight when they drove across Arkansas. They'd left the last place because they couldn't quite catch up with the rent.

"That's how we met Norman Ritz," he said.

"Who could forget Norman Ritz?" she said. She laughed.

Albert loved the sound of his mother's laughter.

"He came stumbling out of that shack by the side of the road like a wild man," she said.

"I was going to run," Albert said.

"He had a glass eye that was a different color than the real one," she said.

"It fell out when he was fixing our car," Albert said.

"I had to go underneath to get it, and he showed me how it went back in."

"He was a nice man," she said. "He wouldn't take any money." She turned the hamburgers over.

Albert stirred the beans. He moved the pot to the side of the grill because they were bubbling. "I'll try harder at school," he said.

He watched her. She looked weary. He could see discouragement in her face.

"I just need things to be a little easier," she said. "That's all I'm asking."

They heard an engine that sounded like a high-speed coffee grinder pull into the clearing by the trailer.

"Who could be coming to visit us?" Elly asked.

They heard the engine die.

Elly started for the front of the trailer.

"Anybody here?" a man's voice called out.

2

THE OVERNIGHT GUEST

Elly went rigid.

Albert saw his mother put her finger to her lips, signaling him to stay quiet.

"Shouldn't leave the front door open," the man's voice said, getting closer. "You never know who might come around."

Albert couldn't remember seeing his mother so upset. He thought it must be his father returning, and he braced himself. He'd never heard a positive word about his father.

"Smells good back here," the voice said.

A tall, brown-skinned old man in a wrinkled seersucker suit, white button-down shirt, and red knit necktie appeared around the corner of the trailer. He was carrying a violin case and a gym bag.

"What are you doing here?" Elly yelled. "Never mind. I don't want to know. I want you to leave. Now!"

The old man stood straight as an athlete. He held his handsome gray-haired head high.

"Hello, Albert," the old man said.

"Who are you?" Albert asked.

"It doesn't matter who he is," Elly said. She turned to the old man. "I want you to go, Wendell. Please. Can you at least do that for me?"

"Sure, Elly," Wendell said. "I can do that." His eyes stayed locked on Albert.

"I'm your grandfather," he said.

"You can't be my grandfather," Albert said. "You're black."

"More on the brown side," Wendell said.

"He's your grandfather," Elly said, "and he's my father, and he's going to say goodbye."

"How can I have a brown grandfather?" Albert looked at the skin on his arm, then at Wendell.

"I'm half African American, half Native American, and half Caucasian," Wendell said.

"That's impossible," Albert said. "You can't be three halves of something."

"Go figure," Wendell said.

"He has no idea who he is," Elly said. "He's never been the same person two weeks in a row his whole life. Time to go, whoever you are." She took her father by the arm.

Wendell smiled at Albert. His eyes crinkled around the corners. They were pale blue, like his grandson's. His teeth were white and straight.

"My mother was half Narragansett Indian," he said. "Most of the rest was Norwegian. My father was Ethiopian and Italian. There's some Irish and Greek in there somewhere too. You're pretty much a walking United Nations."

Wendell looked at Elly. "He's got our side of the family written all over him. You look tired."

"You're making me tired," she said.

"I have a grandfather?" Albert asked, as though he couldn't believe it was possible.

"Call me Wendell," Wendell said.

"How come you knew my name?" Albert asked. "I never saw you before."

"You did once," Wendell said. "When you were too young to remember."

"I never even heard of you," Albert said.

"There are good reasons for that," Wendell said.

"We had an agreement," Elly said.

"It's just this one exception," Wendell said. "What's that cooking?"

"No way," Elly said, remembering the hamburgers. She moved quickly to remove them from the grill.

"He can have half of mine," Albert said. "You're always telling me to be kind to strangers."

"He's not a stranger," Elly said. She put slices of cheese on top of the hamburgers.

"He is to me," Albert said.

"We'll make a new arrangement," Wendell said. His smile was warm enough to melt ice. "After this, you'll never see me again."

"That's what you said last time," Elly said.

Albert brought out a chair and an extra plate from the kitchen. Elly served herself. Albert served Wendell, then himself. They ate in silence. Elly stared straight ahead, like a person eating alone in a restaurant. Albert kept stealing glances at his grandfather, who seemed perfectly at ease with his present set of circumstances.

"Good cheeseburger," Wendell said when he was done. He licked his fingers. "The beans were excellent."

"I cooked the beans," Albert said. "How come my mother's not brown like you? How come I'm not brown?"

16

"Who knows?" Wendell responded. "You shake a bunch of colors together, you have no idea what will come out. You yourself run toward olive. Your mother is on the brighter side. That's the Irish coming to the surface. You've got Mediterranean in you. Why? Does it matter what color I am?"

Albert thought about it for a moment. He looked his grandfather up and down. He wondered what it would be like to be a different color than he was. Blue maybe. Or green.

"No," he said. "It doesn't make any difference what color anybody is. Do you play the violin?" He eyed the case by his grandfather's feet. It was made of deep, rich wood that seemed to glow.

"Not a note," Wendell said.

"Then why do you have a violin case?"

"Why not?" Wendell responded.

"How is the Stradivarius?" Elly asked.

"As ever," Wendell said. "As always."

"What's a Stradivarius?" Albert asked.

"A very old, very rare violin made by Antonio Stradivari, or one of his sons," Wendell said. "They're works of art."

"Why do you have a Stradivarius if you don't play the violin?" Albert asked. "Why do you carry it around?"

"Tell him what's in the case," Elly said.

"You tell him," Wendell said.

"I don't know," Elly said to Albert. "Nobody knows what's inside. He's never let anybody look."

"How come?" Albert asked.

"Your great-grandfather Enrique was a spear carrier for the Metropolitan Opera Company in New York City, island of Manhattan," Wendell said. "His father was Spanish and Moroccan. His mother was Indonesian and Dutch. Your great-granduncle Eduardo was an artist. I have my Stradivarius."

"Tell him what else his great-grandfather Enrique was," Elly said.

"He was a businessman," Wendell said.

"Like you're an astronaut," Elly said.

"If I ever have to fill out a form," Wendell said, "I'd be inclined to put myself down as an entrepreneur."

"Some entrepreneur," Elly said. "Tell your grandson what you do for a living."

"I move around a lot," Wendell said.

"And why is that?" she asked.

"I'm rehabilitated, Elly," Wendell said. "I'm out of it for good."

"And I'm the Queen of Transylvania," Elly said.

"There is royal blood in the family," Wendell said to Albert. "We have a direct connection to Napoleon the

Third through marriage. He was the other Napoleon, the one who widened the streets of Paris."

"Your grandfather is in no way rehabilitated," Elly said to Albert. "He's on the run. He's always on the run."

"Not anymore," Wendell said. "I'm too old. Too slow. I forget things." He turned his attention to Albert.

"Stay away from what you're no good at," he said. "Develop a skill. Be better at it than anybody else."

"The voice of wisdom speaks," Elly said.

Albert thought his grandfather looked old enough to be too worn out to do anything. "Why do you move around a lot?"

"Good question," Elly said.

"This and that," Wendell said.

"You have to move around a lot when you con people out of their money," Elly said.

"I never took ten cents from anybody who couldn't afford it," Wendell said. "I never took a dollar more than I needed. I was never greedy. Greed kills the spirit. No self-respecting person takes more than he needs."

"Rob the rich and give to Wendell," Elly said. "You're a social worker."

"I've been called a lot of things," Wendell said, "but never that. I'm done with it now. All I'm looking for is a little recreation and a place to set myself down."

"Not here," Elly said. She got to her feet.

"I wouldn't ask you something like that," Wendell said. "Besides, right now I'm in pursuit of the country's natural wonders. I was just at Yellowstone. Hard to believe if you haven't seen it with your own eyes. I'd like to stay the night."

"No," Elly said.

"Yes," Albert said.

"If I could use the bathroom," Wendell said, "I'd appreciate it."

"The bathroom and then you're out of here," Elly said.

Wendell picked up his gym bag and violin case and disappeared around the corner of the trailer.

"Why didn't you tell me I had a grandfather?" Albert asked.

"You don't," she said. "Not in any way that matters."

"It matters to me," Albert said.

"He's leaving."

"I don't want him to leave."

"You don't know anything about him."

"That's why I want him to stay."

"He's had his chance. More than one."

"One night."

"No."

"I'm never going to see him again."

"I wish you'd never seen him at all."

"But I have," Albert said, "and now he's going away. I don't care what he did."

"He's a crook," Elly said. "He ran out on me and my mother when I was your age."

"Well, he's not a crook now," Albert said. "I should at least be able to spend one night with him in my life."

"A few hours, Elly," Wendell said as he came back around the corner. He stood there, bag and case in hand, looking frail, like he'd aged ten years in the two minutes he'd been gone.

"I'll be on the road before you wake up," he said. "You'll never see me after that."

"You can have my bed," Albert said. "I'll sleep on the floor."

3

ALBERT PHONES HOME

"I'm in Boise," Albert said.

"Where?" Elly's voice was clouded with sleep.

"Boise. Wendell brought me up to see the Anne Frank Memorial. He said it would be instructive."

Albert looked over at Wendell, who nodded his approval. They were at an outside pay phone. It was early Friday morning.

"We're going to see it as soon as I hang up," Albert continued.

"Don't hang up!" Elly yelled. "I want you to come home right now. I don't want you with him."

"Wendell says it's important to experience places

like the Anne Frank Memorial," Albert said. "He wants to take me to the pioneer museum in Baker City. That's in Oregon."

"I know where Baker City is," Elly said, "and you're not going there or anywhere else with him. I'll take you when I have time. I want you to come home."

"I'm suspended from school," Albert said. "What am I going to do at home except get in trouble?"

"Put Wendell on," she said.

"Morning, Elly," Wendell said smoothly, taking over the phone from Albert. "We were going to let you sleep later, but I got worried you'd get up and see Albert gone without an explanation."

"I am worried!" Albert heard his mother yell at his grandfather, her voice crackling through the earpiece. "I'm sick with worry. I want him back. In the time it takes to drive him here. Which is an hour."

"Or I could show him a few things," Wendell said. "Spend a few days with him. He tells me he can't go back to school until Tuesday."

"Bring him home."

"If that's what you want."

"That's what I want."

"But maybe," Wendell said, like he hadn't heard a word she'd said, "just maybe we'd get something out of it, the two of us, me and your son, if we had the pleasure of each other's company. Let me take him to Seattle. He should see Seattle, Elly. He should stand at the top of the Space Needle. He should walk through the Market. He should eat at a nice restaurant. He should ride on the monorail. He should cross Puget Sound on the ferry at night so he can see what the city looks like coming back. I'll take him to see his grandmother's grave."

Wendell handed the phone to Albert as Elly was screaming "No!"

"You said you wanted a vacation," Albert said. "If you let me go I won't be around to bug you. You can do whatever you want. It's the only chance I'm ever going to have to be with him."

He handed the phone back to Wendell.

"I'll have him back Monday afternoon," Wendell said. "I promise I won't do anything wrong. All we're going to do is have a little fun."

"Why should I trust you?" she asked. Albert could tell she was giving way.

"Because he's my grandson," Wendell said. "I wouldn't let anything happen to my grandson. Just because we have problems doesn't mean I don't have feelings. I'll behave myself."

Wendell winked at Albert. "I think we sold her," he said.

"Monday afternoon," Elly said. "If he's not back here by four o'clock, I'm calling the police."

"Four o'clock it is," Wendell said. He handed Albert the phone.

"Thanks, Mom," Albert said. "You won't be sorry."

"I'm already sorry," Elly said. "I'm only doing this because you think it's so important. You'll have to learn like the rest of us. I want you to call me every day so I know you're all right. So I know he hasn't lost you in a card game."

"That's funny," Albert said.

"No it's not," she said.

"I want you to soak your feet," Albert said. "I want you to sleep as much as you can. I don't want you to worry."

"I'll worry all I want," she said. "I'll worry until I see you. Be careful. Have a good time. If he starts any monkey business, call me."

"No monkey business," Albert said.

"I love you," she said, then hung up.

Albert felt an immediate prickle of worry. What if she was right? What if his grandfather was up to no good?

As his heart started thumping, he told himself there was nothing to be concerned about. After all, how much trouble could a twelve-year-old boy and a seventy-two-year-old man get into?

4

WORDS

Albert and Wendell studied the statue of the small girl. She was standing on a chair, peering out the window of her attic hideout. She held her diary behind her back.

"She was fifteen when she died at Bergen-Belsen," Wendell said. "That was a Nazi concentration camp. She kept the diary when she was in hiding with her family before that. In Amsterdam. She wrote about their lives and how she felt about things. Her diary survived. You should read it."

Albert wondered how much the statue looked like the real Anne Frank.

"She saw the better side of things," Wendell said. "This whole park is dedicated to her."

Albert turned to take it in. The grassy areas mixed with curving walkways that were lined with benches where you could sit and study the stone walls engraved with quotations about peace and human dignity and the struggle for freedom.

Wendell started walking. Albert followed. They studied the words of Sojourner Truth and Mahatma Gandhi and Martin Luther King, Jr., and Nelson Mandela and Chief Joseph and Eleanor Roosevelt and Haim Ginott and many others. The words of Anne Frank were everywhere.

"How do you know about this place?" Albert asked.

"It's something everybody should know," Wendell said.

As Wendell's ancient camper bus, which was painted several shades of red and wheezed like it had asthma, headed north on Route 84 out of Boise, Albert considered the words he'd read and the people who'd written them. They were from everywhere in the world, Wendell had told him. Most of them were dead.

"Words outlive people," Wendell had said.

Albert remembered most of all the words written by

Anne Frank: "In spite of everything, I still believe that people are truly good at heart."

He saw Wendell watching him. "I can't believe I'm doing this," he said.

"Life is full of surprises," Wendell said. "Your mother is a trusting person. She gets that from her mother. You bring any money with you?"

"Six dollars," Albert said. "It's all I have."

Wendell held out his hand. "It goes in the general fund. I'll pay you back later."

Albert took the six one-dollar bills from his pants pocket and gave them to his grandfather.

"I was in prison once," Wendell said.

"Why?" Albert asked. He tried to picture his grandfather behind bars.

"Don't tell your mother," Wendell said. "She has enough problems."

"What did you do?"

"It was a mistake. I've done a few things I might have gone to jail for, but this wasn't one of them. They got the wrong man. I did time for something I didn't do. Even so, I figured it paid whatever debt I might owe society. Sort of canceled things out."

"What did they say you did?"

"Said I wrote some bad checks for a lot of money," Wendell said. "Which wasn't my style. But some certain somebody started using my modus operandi in other respects and I couldn't prove it wasn't me. So off I went."

"Who really did it?"

"That is the one unresolved piece of business I have left," Wendell said. "Don't leave behind unfinished business if you can help it. Try to keep harmony and balance in your life."

Albert digested all that as best he could.

"Jail stinks," Wendell said. "Although it's clearly where some people belong. I was in when your mother married your father."

"Do you know anything about my father?"

"Ask your mother," Wendell said.

"It's a sore subject with her," Albert said. "The only time I ever hear her swear is when I ask her about him."

"You sure you want to know?"

"It's better than not knowing," Albert said.

"After I got out of jail I found out where your mother was living. I found your father at a bar. He had no idea who I was. We had a talk. I wouldn't say I liked him. I thought your mother made a mistake. On the other hand, if they hadn't got married, you wouldn't have been born and we wouldn't be having this conversation and that would be a shame."

"What was he like?"

"He was stupid."

"What did he do that was stupid?"

"He thought it was okay to live off your mother's wages while he sat around drinking beer and getting fat."

"I don't remember him."

"I only met him that once," Wendell said. "But I kept tabs on him."

"Did you tell my mother?"

"Never tell a woman something she doesn't want to hear. That's been my experience. I hadn't seen your mother in a long time. She wouldn't have been happy to see me. After you were born I came by. She let me stay an hour. Your father was already gone. He was stupid because he chased after other women. Maybe you shouldn't hear all this."

"If you don't tell me, who will?"

"Your mother, if she wants to. Anyway, that's what I know."

"Did he run away?"

"She threw him out. He was a bum of the first order."

"Am I a bum of the first order?" Albert asked.

"Not for a minute," Wendell said. "You're a thousand times smarter and you have a winning personality and you're better looking. That's just three ways. I could list a hundred if you're interested."

"What's his name?"

"Boyer," Wendell said. "Randolph Boyer."

"Then why am I named Rosegarden?"

"Because your mother went back to her original name after she divorced him. She had yours changed by a judge."

"What happened to him?"

"I heard once he moved to Florida," Wendell said. "Maybe an alligator got him."

"Are you a bum of the first order?"

"I'm ashamed of some of what I've done, but not most of it," Wendell said. "When I left my wife and your mother, I was running from the law. I kept running so they wouldn't bother my family. Be careful what you get good at, Albert. When the weekend is over, you can decide for yourself what I am."

"I'm not good at anything," Albert said.

Wendell offered his grandson a broad smile.

"You're not your father and you're not me. You're you."

They passed a sign for the town of Fruitland, population 2,400. They crossed the Snake River into Oregon.

5
AN OLD COWBOY AND A THREE-LEGGED DOG

They pulled off Route 84 at Baker City.

"Gold was discovered here in 1861," Wendell said.

They made their way through the town's historic district. Albert's eyes widened when he saw the Geiser Grand Hotel.

"Looks just like it did when the gold flowed," Wendell said.

Albert imagined himself running through the streets, a gold prospector filthy rich with a new strike. He saw the sign for the National Historic Oregon Trail Interpretive Center.

"That's the pioneer museum," Wendell said.

A busload of tourists was disembarking when they got there. The parking lot was nearly full.

"Look around," Wendell said as they climbed down from the camper bus. "I'll be back shortly."

Albert watched Wendell walk off. He gave a cursory look at some old wagon ruts and a genuine pioneer wagon being pulled by a pair of oxen, then ran after his grandfather.

He followed him into a building, to a display showing how people lived during Baker City's boom times. He saw Wendell shake hands with an old man who was wearing boots and a string tie and a cowboy hat that looked like a horse had sat on it. He moved closer until he could hear.

"How's the Stradivarius?" the old cowboy asked.

"As ever," Wendell said. "As always. You reach everybody?"

"I sure did," the old cowboy said. "They're all waiting on your arrival. You're looking good, Wendell."

"I am good," Wendell said. "How about you?"

"I was ninety-three last week," the old cowboy said. "Far as I know, all my parts are still working. Let me know how it goes?"

"I'll send you a money order," Wendell said.

"That'll do it," the old cowboy said. "Take care of yourself."

"You too," Wendell said.

The old cowboy went off in one direction and Wendell in another.

Albert ran as fast as he could and just beat his grandfather back to the camper bus.

"Seen enough?" Wendell asked.

"My mother said she'd bring me here sometime," Albert said. "The rest can wait until then."

"We'll gas up," Wendell said.

They pulled into the first station they came to. Albert jumped out and unscrewed the gas cap.

"Hey! You can't do that!" A kid came running out of the office.

"I can if I want to," Albert said.

"You can't pump your own gas," the kid said. He blocked Albert from getting to the nozzle.

"You can't tell me what to do!" Albert yelled. "It's my grandfather's bus. Get out of my way!"

"He's right," Wendell said. "You can't pump the gas."

"Why not?" Albert yelled. "I do it at home."

"Because the law in Oregon says you can't," Wendell said.

"How come?"

"Who knows?"

Wendell gave the kid ten dollars, then put a hand on Albert's shoulder and guided him away.

"Never get excited at people," Wendell said quietly when they were off a few steps. "You stop listening when you get excited. You stop watching. It gives people an advantage."

"What kind of law says you can't pump your own gas?" Albert asked.

"There are laws against everything," Wendell said. He stopped and looked down at his grandson. "We have a couple of days together. It's the only time like it we'll ever have. Relax and enjoy it. So you can remember liking it later."

The kid checked the oil and tires and cleaned the windshield and back window while Albert and Wendell used the men's room. As they were leaving, Albert told the kid he was sorry. The kid said not to worry about it.

"Maybe it's the law because it keeps people from losing jobs," Albert said.

They headed north on Route 84 again. They made their way fitfully through the Blue Mountains. The camper bus struggled up one long ascent after another, then felt like it was going to tip over on the way down.

"What was my mother like when she was my age?" Albert asked when they were finally driving on flat road.

"She asked a lot of questions," Wendell said. "She got in trouble at school. She had a big heart. Still does. She had a bicycle, you'd have thought it was a pony the way she took care of it. She had the best smile I ever saw. Still does. She should have kept going to school. She's all untapped potential, your mother. She's got everything she needs but confidence."

They pulled off the highway before they got to Pendleton and drove parallel to it for a short while, then turned off onto a dirt and gravel road that took them to a cabin set among some trees behind a hill. A hundred yards away cattle were grazing.

Wendell honked the horn and the door of the cabin opened and a three-legged dog that was hardly larger than a softball came ripping out, followed by a man the size of a bear.

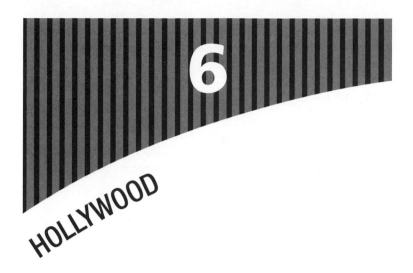

Albert was transfixed by the tiny three-legged dog that waited for him as he stepped down from the camper bus.

The dog eyed him with a steady gaze.

Albert squatted.

The dog—it was his left front leg that was missing—bobbed his way to Albert, sniffed, then sat. The dog was sandy-colored with short, straight hair and whiskers.

Wendell and the bear of a man hugged.

"Big Royal," Wendell said.

"Wendell Rosegarden," Big Royal said.

Big Royal had long hair and bushy eyebrows.

"Albert, this is my half-brother-in-law, Big Royal," Wendell said.

"Good to meet you," Albert said. "What's your dog's name?"

"Hollywood," Big Royal said.

"How come he's missing a leg?" Albert asked.

"Cancer," Big Royal said. "I carved him a new one from wood, but he chewed it off. Get your stuff and come inside."

Albert collected his backpack. Hollywood watched.

"How's the Stradivarius?" Big Royal asked as Wendell grabbed his violin case and gym bag.

"As ever," Wendell said. "As always."

"Sometimes I think you have a violin in there," Big Royal said.

"You never know," Wendell said.

The cabin was one big room, which was the kitchen, dining room, and living room combined, plus two bedrooms and a bathroom. The ceiling was twenty feet high. Fans hung from beams, swooshing quietly. At the far end of the big room was a worktable with a large black manual typewriter sitting on it.

"How come your dog's name is Hollywood?" Albert asked. He was parked on a stool watching Big Royal and Wendell mix martinis. Hollywood sat on the counter watching him.

"Because he's a bad actor," Big Royal said.

"He was a movie dog," Wendell said.

"He was in the movies?" Albert looked at Hollywood like he might have missed something the first time around. "This dog?"

"He was in one movie," Big Royal said. "For one day. He bit the director, producer, studio executive, and leading man all before lunch. I quit the business, bought the dog, changed his name to Hollywood, and left town before the afternoon was over."

Hollywood jumped off the counter onto Albert's lap. It was like having a small missile come at you.

Albert petted him.

Hollywood licked Albert's face.

"Big Royal used to write for the movies," Wendell said. "Big Royal has a way with words."

"Action-adventure," Big Royal said. "Cops and robbers."

The dog could fit in my pocket, Albert thought. Its expression was as intense as his own. He figured its ancestry was equally mysterious.

They had steak for dinner, with fried potatoes. That was followed by large slabs of coconut cake. Hollywood had a little of each, eating from a bowl which he pushed across the floor so it was next to Albert's feet.

Afterward they sat in stuffed chairs. Wendell and

Big Royal sipped at mugs of coffee. Albert rested a gentle hand on Hollywood's back.

"What's that on the table?" Albert asked.

Big Royal turned to see what Albert was talking about.

"He means your typewriter," Wendell said.

"It's a manual," Big Royal said. "No electricity required."

"What's it for?" Albert asked.

"Not much anymore," Big Royal said. "I wrote my scripts on it."

"How's it work?"

"I'll show you," Big Royal said.

Albert scooped Hollywood up in one hand and watched while Big Royal rolled a piece of paper into the machine and lined it up.

"Now here's what makes the typewriter the greatest writing machine ever invented," Big Royal said. He struck a key. The key went *wap!* The letter *A* appeared on the piece of paper.

"You strike the *A*, you get an *A*," Big Royal said. "Amazing, ain't it? Want to try?"

Albert struck the keys that spelled his name.

"The typewriter is called Little Royal," Wendell said.

"There's no spell-check," Albert said.

Big Royal laughed. "There are letters and numbers and punctuation marks. Everything else is up to you."

Albert listened to Wendell and Big Royal talk about a bunch of people he'd never heard of. He started nodding off and decided it was time for bed. Hollywood joined him. The dog settled on one side of the pillow.

As he started to fall into the darkness of sleep, Albert heard the keys of Little Royal striking paper. He heard the murmur of Wendell's and Big Royal's voices discussing what was being written.

Albert smelled bacon and eggs. He blinked several times and saw that Hollywood was six inches away, watching him. They appraised each other for a while.

"How you doing?" Albert asked.

Hollywood yawned.

Albert wondered what dogs thought about.

Hollywood licked his face.

"Let's go eat," Albert said.

Big Royal and Wendell greeted them with cheery "good mornings." Big Royal asked Albert to take Hollywood outside. Breakfast would be ready when they got back. "It doesn't take him long," Big Royal said.

Hollywood sniffed at this and that until he found the exact spot he was looking for. He shifted his weight slightly forward on his right front leg, lifted his right rear leg an inch off the ground, and did his business, a very serious expression attached to his face, as though it required all his concentration to make this happen. Albert tried not to laugh but couldn't help it. When they returned, Albert sat down at the table. Hollywood sat on the chair next to him.

The boy ate two fried eggs, three strips of bacon, two slices of toast with strawberry jam, and drank a large glass of milk. The dog shared his meal.

"You sure you want to do this?" Wendell asked Big Royal.

"A dog deserves a holiday like everybody else," Big Royal said.

"What are you talking about?" Albert asked.

"Hollywood's coming with us to Seattle," Wendell said. "Big Royal's letting you borrow him."

Albert and Hollywood looked at each other.

"There's only one rule," Big Royal said. "He never gets left alone. You take him everywhere."

"Okay," Albert said without hesitating. He'd never had a dog and this one certainly wasn't what he'd have chosen if he was going to get one, but he liked him. The thought of them being together for a few days made Albert happy.

"You can carry him in your pocket," Big Royal said. "Slip him in backward so his head sticks out. He'll hide when you go into any public place. He won't make a sound."

They thanked Big Royal for putting them up.

"We'll see you Monday afternoon," Wendell said.

"I'll be here," Big Royal said.

Hollywood bounced over to Big Royal, stood there for a moment looking up at him, then bounced back to Albert.

"Why are you letting him come with me?" Albert asked.

"He's the one who did the deciding," Big Royal said.

Wendell turned the camper bus around and they headed for the highway. Albert shifted in his seat and studied his surroundings. For all that he'd spent his life living in confined spaces, he'd never seen anything like it. The sides were paneled with wood. Venetian blinds covered the windows. A thick green carpet covered the floor. The ceiling was painted blue, with white puffy clouds set into it. An ice chest, a shelf of books, a hand-crank radio, a cushioned seat, a folding table, and a lamp filled out the rest.

"It's a good way to travel if you don't want to be noticed," Wendell said.

A few miles north of Pendleton, they pulled off to visit Albert's grandmother Lucille.

"She was Guatemalan, Danish, and Seminole Indian," Wendell said. They were standing by her grave. The cemetery was small and fenced in.

"Her family is buried here," Wendell said. "This is their corner. It's full."

"I'm related to all these people?" Albert asked.

"You have a grandmother, great-grandmother and great-grandfather, and some granduncles and grandaunts in the ground here. I never knew any of them except Lucille. I met her on a train. In the dining car. I spilled my soup when I saw her."

"Did you love her?"

"Still do," Wendell said. "She had a temper like fireworks. She'd explode. The air would fill with light and heat. Then it was all over and she'd laugh."

"Was she pretty?"

"Stunning," Wendell said. "Dignified in manner. Strong as steel. Smart. She deserved better than me."

Wendell seemed to have a fast answer to every question.

Albert felt Hollywood stir in his hand and set him down. The dog hobbled away from the family plot, focused his attention on the task at hand, and peed next to a bush.

"He couldn't fill a thimble," Wendell said.

Hollywood returned, and Albert picked him up. They stood another minute looking at the grave.

"We have to go," Wendell said. He touched the top of Lucille's marker, then headed back to the camper bus.

Albert took a last look around, then followed.

They got off Route 84 onto Route 82. A short while later they crossed the Columbia River at Umatilla and entered the state of Washington.

"Washington became a state in 1889," Albert said. "The capital is Olympia. Oregon became a state in 1859. The capital is Salem. Idaho became a state in 1890. The capital is Boise. Want to hear the rest of them?"

"Absolutely," Wendell said.

Albert knocked off the remaining forty-seven states with the dates of their founding and their capitals in alphabetical order. "I like geography," he said when he was done.

At Yakima they crossed the Naches River. It was getting on toward noon. Hollywood was sleeping.

"You like school?"

Albert shrugged his shoulders.

"You've been to a bunch of them," Wendell said.

How did he know, Albert wondered.

"I've lived a bunch of places," Albert said. "Hepworth, Pennsylvania. Permanent, Ohio. Livermore,

Wisconsin. Humphollow, Oklahoma. Mountain View, Idaho. Those are the ones I remember."

"I always felt trapped in school," Wendell said. "You're in a room. The door is closed. You can't get out."

"It depends," Albert said.

"On what?"

"On who the teacher is," Albert said.

"Nothing like a good teacher," Wendell said.

"I like to read," Albert said. "I like writing and history. I don't mind math."

"The important thing in an education is learning to see the overall picture," Wendell said. "What are the questions I should be asking? Where do I find the answers? What do you want out of life, Albert?"

"How should I know? I'm a kid."

"Start thinking about it," Wendell said. He pointed out the window. "Look at that!"

Up ahead of them Albert saw Mount Rainier and Mount Adams, towering above the peaks around them like spires, their tops capped with ice, even in late summer.

"Those two are alive," Wendell said. "Filled to the brim with fire."

They stopped in Ellensburg to buy turkey sandwiches and fill the tank. This time Albert got to do the pumping. Then they were heading west on I-90 toward Seattle.

"Tell me about your mother," Wendell said while they were eating.

"She comes home late at night," Albert said, feeding a piece of turkey to Hollywood. "Then sometimes she can't sleep. I hear her walking around. Sometimes she doesn't fall asleep until it gets light out."

"That runs contrary to the normal human twenty-four-hour cycle," Wendell said.

"She says it's the most money she can make," Albert said.

"And that's not much, is it?"

"It couldn't be too much," Albert said, "or we wouldn't be living like we are."

"She seeing anybody?" Wendell asked. He glanced at his grandson. "She going out with any men?"

"Not lately," Albert said. "She used to. None of them lasted very long."

"A man can wear a woman down," Wendell said.

"We go to the movies sometimes," Albert said. "Sometimes we go to Crystal's for pie. We're mostly at the trailer together when she's not working and I'm not at school."

"She should have a better life."

"I'm going to take care of that someday," Albert said.

They made their way up into the Cascades and over Snoqualmie Pass. They passed North Bend and started hitting traffic. Hollywood was lying on Albert's shoulder, looking out the window.

"Tell me about you," Albert said.

"What do you want to know?"

"What have you done besides go to jail?"

"I was an air-taxi pilot once," Wendell said, without missing a beat. "I flew a twin-engine job between a bunch of those small islands in the Caribbean. I flew tourists, deadbeats, tax dodgers, people on the run in general, people looking for people on the run . . . The second time I crashed I decided to find a new career."

"You crashed in an airplane?"

"Walked away without a scratch both times. I heard the message."

"What'd you do after that?"

"You're not interested in what I did before that?"

"Before and after," Albert said.

"If you're talking about situations where I had to work, I was a short-order cook, a tour guide, a bartender, a barista, a deckhand, a fisherman, a housepainter, and a card dealer."

"You did all that and you never played the violin?" Albert asked.

"Never," Wendell said. "I'm tone-deaf."

They crossed the the Lacey V. Murrow Floating Bridge. Albert saw the spires of Seattle's skyscrapers rising up in front of him.

"There it is," Wendell said. "The Emerald City. This is going to be the most fun you've ever had."

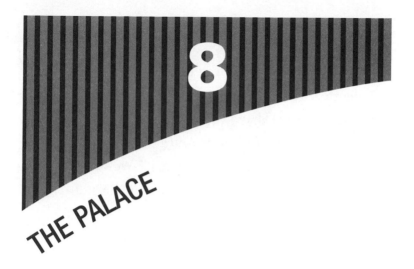

THE PALACE

Albert and Hollywood had their heads stuck out the camper bus window trying to see everything at once. Sirens wailed. Jackhammers slammed into concrete. The streets were filled with traffic. Albert had never seen so many people. He craned his neck to find the tops of buildings. In front of a department store he saw eight musicians wearing straw hats and playing flutes and pipes. At a traffic light he watched a policeman on a horse ride across the intersection. A train that slid along on one rail hummed by overhead.

"There's the Palace," Wendell announced, making a right at a red light.

Albert studied the square stone building. A green-

and-gold canopy covered its entrance. A large man in a green-and-gold uniform stood guard while a small army scurried about helping the hotel's patrons, opening doors, carrying luggage, and parking cars. The horseshoe-shaped driveway was lined with flags and crowded with cars and taxis and limousines.

"It was built in the early 1900s," Wendell said as they drove by. "Restored to its former glory a decade ago. The best hotel in town."

They turned into the alley behind the Palace and stopped at the delivery entrance.

"Let's go," Wendell said, grabbing his gym bag and violin case.

Albert slipped his backpack on his shoulder and put Hollywood in his pocket. He figured it was better if nobody saw the dog until he knew it was safe.

"Why are we getting out here?" he asked.

"This is where we're staying," Wendell said.

A man in a hotel uniform stepped out onto the loading platform. "Up here," he said.

Another uniformed man wearing a Mariners baseball cap came out, got into the camper bus, and drove it away.

"Where's he going with our bus?" Albert asked.

"He's a valet. He's parking it," Wendell said. "That's his job."

"It's good to see you, Wendell," the man on the platform said. "You're right on time." The man was Wendell's age. He was short and sturdy.

"Albert, I want you to meet Willie Two," Wendell said. "Willie Two is an old friend. He's a bellman. That means he helps hotel guests with their luggage."

Willie Two shook Albert's hand. "You have a dog in your pocket," he said.

"That's Hollywood," Albert said.

"He's on loan from Big Royal," Wendell said.

"This way," Willie Two said. "How is Big Royal?"

"He's good," Wendell said.

Willie Two led them through a door into the bowels of the hotel. They made their way down a long corridor, past the boiler room and storage rooms and the laundry and kitchen. They stepped into a big, beat-up cage. A freight elevator, his grandfather explained. Willie Two pressed a button, and up they went.

"How was the ride in?" Willie Two asked.

"Pleasant," Wendell said. "The family is well?"

"Everybody's great," Willie Two said. He looked at Albert and smiled.

They got off the elevator at the top floor. Willie Two led them down a hallway that was covered with drop cloths and lined with cans of paint, buckets of brushes, and a stack of ladders.

"Everything will be cleaned up by dinner," Willie Two said. "We'll have it looking perfect."

Willie Two unlocked the double doors at the end of the hall and threw them open.

"Your rooms," he said.

Albert turned a slow 360 degrees in the middle of the entry. The walls were covered with a mural of a farm and all its animals and the people who lived there.

"The painters won't be back until seven o'clock Monday morning," Willie Two said. "You have to be out no later than five."

He handed Wendell a cell phone. "It's prepaid," Willie Two said. "All the numbers you need are taped to the back. I'll let everybody know you're here."

"Well done," Wendell said.

"See you shortly," Willie Two said to Albert.

He handed Wendell the keys to the suite. "How's the Stradivarius?"

"As ever," Wendell said. "As always."

Willie Two nodded and left.

"Why is he called Willie Two?" Albert asked.

"His father was Willie One," Wendell said.

"Why are we staying here if they're painting?"

"Because the price is right," Wendell said.

"Why did we come in the back door?"

"To avoid the lines at the check-in desk," Wendell said. "All the important people use the back door. It's the VIP entrance. Pick a bedroom. Wash up. We've got places to go, appointments to keep."

Albert and Hollywood wandered down a hall, past the dining room and living room and entertainment room, which Albert stopped to inspect because it had a pool table and the largest television set he'd ever seen. He found a bedroom with a four-poster bed and glass doors that led to a balcony looking out over the city. The balcony was bigger than the trailer he and Elly lived in.

"Will this be okay for a couple of days?" he asked Hollywood.

The dog made a small growling sound, which Albert took to be a sign of approval.

9

SHAVE AND A HAIRCUT

"A little off the top and neaten the sides," Wendell said. "How about you, Albert?"

"A little off the top and neaten the sides," Albert said.

"Appearance helps your confidence," Wendell said. "Confidence matters."

Albert and Wendell were sitting side by side in Eddie and Eddie's barbershop. Eddie and Eddie were father and son. They were both bald. The shop had two chairs. There was a red-and-white-striped pole outside the door. The air was permanently scented with talcum powder and Bay Rum. The Closed sign was hanging in the window.

Eddie the younger brushed the hair off the back of Albert's neck.

Eddie the elder shaved Wendell's face, working the straight razor in slow, steady strokes.

When they were done, Albert and Wendell examined themselves in the mirror.

"From the shoulders up," Wendell said, "we are outstanding."

They thanked the two Eddies and left.

"How come we didn't have to pay?" Albert asked when they were outside.

"I was Eddie the elder's first customer," Wendell said. They headed off down the sidewalk.

At Mr. Jay's, purveyor of fine European men's shoes, they sat side by side in new socks. Mr. Jay slipped rich brown Italian loafers on their feet.

"Walk around," Mr. Jay said. He wore wire-rim glasses. A gray mustache was nestled beneath his slightly bulbous nose.

Albert and Wendell walked back and forth on the carpet.

They stood looking down at the mirror that was angled to show them their feet.

"From the ankles down we look terrific," Albert said.

"We'll take them," Wendell said.

At Nelson's menswear store Albert was introduced to Johnny Lark, who sold suits. He was slightly built.

The crease in his trousers was sharp enough to slice bread.

"Two suits each," Johnny Lark said, referring to a list Wendell had handed over. "Two dress shirts each. Two ties each. Two pocket handkerchiefs each. One belt each. Two sets of underwear each. I have that right?"

"To the last button," Wendell said.

"Why are we getting new clothes?" Albert asked.

"We want to make a good impression," Wendell said.

"On who?"

"Time will tell."

"Why do we need new underwear?"

"We're rebuilding from the ground up," Wendell said.

Albert stood on a platform surrounded by mirrors. Hollywood sat by his feet.

Johnny Lark worked his tape measure like a magician works a deck of cards. He wrote down Albert's height and arm length and leg length and the girth of his waist and hips and chest and neck.

"Give him an inside pocket on the jackets strong enough to hold the dog," Wendell said.

Then it was Wendell's turn to be measured.

"Not too formal with the accessories," Wendell said.

"I was thinking of the quietly prosperous look," Johnny Lark said.

"That's the best kind," Wendell said.

"I'll deliver everything personally," Johnny Lark said. "How's the Stradivarius?"

"As ever," Wendell said. "As always."

They left without paying.

10
THE WIZARD OF NOSY

Saturday evening Albert and Wendell entered the living room of their hotel suite wearing identical summer-weight double-breasted light gray suits, pale yellow shirts, black knit neckties, and polka-dot pocket handkerchiefs. Hollywood was inside Albert's jacket, in the reinforced pocket.

Willie Two and Johnny Lark got to their feet. They looked the boy and his grandfather up and down. They walked slowly around them.

"We have a couple of winners here," Willie Two said.

"You outdid yourself," Wendell said to Johnny Lark.

"Sometimes I surprise even myself," Johnny Lark said. Everything he'd brought had fit them perfectly.

Wendell inspected Albert.

Albert inspected Wendell.

"Wear these when you're coming and going inside the hotel," Willie Two said. He handed them each an employee ID card. "If anybody asks, you're training for the front desk."

"I'm twelve," Albert said. "Nobody will believe I'm training for anything."

"They'll believe you in that suit," Johnny Lark said. "You could tell them you're the new governor in that suit and they'd believe you."

"We're off to see the wizard," Wendell said.

"What wizard?" Albert asked.

"The wizard of nosy," Wendell said.

"Where is he?" Albert asked.

"Not always easy to say," Wendell said. "But we're going to have the best dinner you've ever eaten looking for him."

Wendell picked up the violin case. Albert made sure Hollywood was tucked in safely.

"Good luck," Willie Two said.

"Knock 'em dead," Johnny Lark said.

Albert and Wendell took the freight elevator, then

made their way to the loading dock. A limousine and uniformed driver were waiting for them. The driver was short and wide, with spiked red hair.

"Good evening, Mr. Rosegarden," she said in a deep, gravelly voice.

"Good evening, Carmen," Wendell said.

"How are you, Wendell?" she asked, smiling, giving him a big kiss.

"Excellent and getting better," Wendell said. "I want you to meet Albert."

"I'm glad to know you," Carmen said, shaking his hand, nearly lifting him off the ground. She was built like a weight lifter. "Ready to go?"

"I am," Albert said.

"As ready as I'll ever be," Wendell said.

Carmen opened the rear door, and they stepped inside.

"How's the Stradivarius?" she asked.

"As ever," Wendell said. "As always."

"Good," she said. She closed the door and got in behind the wheel.

"How come people keep asking you about the Stradivarius?" Albert asked.

"Force of habit," Wendell said.

"What's your pleasure?" Carmen asked. "We have a few minutes."

"Circle around so Albert can see the new library," Wendell said. "Then take us by the stadiums and waterfront."

"You got it," Carmen said. She closed the glass partition that separated the front of the limousine from the back.

Albert bounced up and down on the seat. Hollywood stuck his head out to see what was going on.

"Not bad, huh?" Wendell said. "Not bad at all."

Albert looked over at his grandfather, who seemed younger all of a sudden. He wasn't such an old man anymore.

"Why are we dressed like this and riding in such a long car?" he asked.

"It's a limousine," Wendell said. "Which is good when you want people to pay attention. This is one of those times."

"Why?"

"You ask more questions than your mother."

"Why is this one of those times?"

"It's a matter of presentation," Wendell said. "If we look like we don't need anything, people will think we don't want anything. That gives us an advantage. Have fun, Albert. Enjoy yourself."

"How come you know Carmen and Willie Two and Johnny Lark and Eddie and Eddie and Mr. Jay?"

"We met here and there. Doing this and that. I know quite a few people."

"How come we never have to pay for anything?"

"You always pay, Albert. Remember that. One way or another there's always a price. In our case, prior arrangements were made. Hit that moonroof button over there."

Wendell pointed.

Albert pressed the button.

The moonroof opened.

"Come on," Wendell said. He stood so that his head stuck up through the opening.

Albert stood on the seat and joined his grandfather. Hollywood stuck his nose into the air.

They drove past the library, which gleamed like a gem in the glow of a warm evening sun. They passed the two ball fields, then drove along Alaskan Way. A ferry was docking. The sidewalks and shops and tour boats and clam bars were packed with tourists. They swung back toward the center of town.

Lights were coming on in the dusk; the white window lights of apartments, the reds and blues and greens and yellows and oranges of neon signs, the flashing, twinkly lights that filled the branches of trees that lined the avenue.

"It looks like magic," Albert said.

"It is magic," Wendell said.

The limousine pulled to the curb, and Carmen jumped out and opened the door. The crowd milling about in front of Crombie's turned its attention to Albert and Wendell as they emerged.

"Who are they?" Albert heard somebody whisper.

"Who's the kid?"

"I think I saw him in a movie."

A man in a tuxedo hurried out of the restaurant and took their arms and escorted Albert and Wendell past the line waiting to get in.

"Wendell, I've never seen you looking so good," the man in the tuxedo said.

"Hugo, I've never seen you looking so good," Wendell said.

Hugo checked out the violin case. "As ever, as always?"

"Couldn't have said it better myself," Wendell said. "This is Albert. His dog, Hollywood, is in his pocket. Albert, this is Hugo. Hugo runs the joint."

"You look just like your grandfather," Hugo said.

He escorted them through a set of etched-glass doors. The dining room buzzed with conversation and laughter and the quiet jazz being played by a trio. The place was jumping.

Hugo brought them to a banquette which was toward the back and off to one side. "An unobstructed view from here," he said to Wendell. "Gloria will be taking care of you."

"What can I say?" Wendell said.

"For you, Wendell, anything," Hugo said. He hurried off.

A moment later a fresh-faced, blond-haired young woman dressed in black appeared. She had a red ribbon in her hair.

"Nice to see you, Mr. Rosegarden," she said to Wendell.

"Hello, Gloria," Wendell said. "This is Albert."

"Hi," Gloria said to Albert, like she'd been waiting all her life to meet him.

Albert's mouth nearly dropped open. She was hardly taller than he was and couldn't have been more than twenty, which he didn't consider that much older.

"I'm Hugo's niece," she said. She smiled.

Albert thought he might fall off his chair.

"I go to college when I'm not doing this," she said. "What would you like to drink?"

"Pink lemonade," Albert said. "If you have it."

"For you, the bartender will make it," Gloria said. She had a tiny gap between her two front teeth.

Wendell ordered a glass of champagne.

Albert watched his grandfather look around the

restaurant. He was aware that Wendell was studying every face, taking a picture of each one before moving on. He saw people glancing at them and knew they were being talked about.

Hollywood's nose twitched this way and that as he took in the atmosphere from inside Albert's jacket.

Gloria returned with their drinks.

Wendell ordered oysters, a green salad, and a filet mignon, rare.

"Filet mignon is French for 'dainty fillet.' It's the best cut of beef you can buy," Wendell said.

"Would it be all right if I had a shrimp cocktail?" Albert asked.

"Whatever you want," Wendell said.

"I'll have a shrimp cocktail," Albert said to Gloria. "Then maybe I could have another shrimp cocktail after that, instead of a salad. Then I'll have another shrimp cocktail after that when he's having his filet mignon."

"Three shrimp cocktails," Gloria said. "Each one bigger than the one before. I love shrimp." She went off to place their order.

Wendell took another quick scan of the room, then lifted his glass. "Here's to the weekend."

"Here's to the weekend," Albert said.

They clinked glasses.

Wendell took another visual survey.

Albert wondered how all this had happened to him. And why? Two days ago he hadn't even known about Wendell Rosegarden. Two days ago he'd been stuck in Mountain View with no prospect of anything exciting happening to him. Now he was dressed in a suit, with a dog in his pocket, sitting in the best restaurant in the biggest city he'd ever been to. He wondered what was next.

"I heard you were dead," a lifeless voice said.

Albert saw a man in a dark suit and shirt approaching their table. His short hair was as dark as his clothes. Albert turned quickly to look at his grandfather, who was smiling.

"Some days I feel like it," Wendell said. "I heard you moved on."

"I come and go," the man said. He looked at Albert with an expression that matched his voice.

"Albert," Wendell said, "this gentleman is Reo Bascom. Before I retired, we were competitors."

"You're retired?" Reo Bascom asked like he didn't believe it.

"Happens to the best of us," Wendell said. "I slowed down a step. I take a nap in the afternoon. I'm feeling my age."

"You don't look retired," Reo Bascom said.

"My advice is to go out at the top of your game," Wendell said. "That's what I did."

Reo Bascom considered this for the better part of a second.

"How's the Stradivarius?" he asked when he was ready to proceed. He tried to make it sound like he didn't care, like it was a courtesy.

But Albert could tell from the little bit of edge at the very end of the question that Reo Bascom cared a great deal.

"As ever," Albert blurted out. "As always."

If Wendell was surprised by Albert's outburst, he gave no indication. Albert was stunned. He hadn't meant to say anything.

Reo Bascom eyed Albert, then focused on Wendell.

"You look like you cashed out big time," he said.

"I invested," Wendell said. "I put something aside for a stormy day. There's no health plan or pension in our line of work. How's business?"

"Business is business," Reo Bascom said.

"He's being modest," Wendell said to Albert. "Reo is the best. He's known as the wizard."

"So, what happens to the Stradivarius now that you're retired?" Reo Bascom asked. "Not that I care."

Albert saw Reo Bascom's eyes flick to the violin case, then back to Wendell.

Wendell sipped his champagne.

Albert sipped his pink lemonade.

"I'll give you a thousand for a look inside the case right now," Reo Bascom said. "To satisfy an old curiosity."

Albert nearly choked. He almost blew pink lemonade out his nose.

"You know better than that," Wendell said.

"Two thousand," Reo Bascom said. "One look. It will just be between us."

"It's an unlikely scenario," Wendell said.

"Unlikely," Albert said, surprising himself again.

"Albert's my right-hand man," Wendell said. "My adviser."

Reo Bascom took a longer look at Albert.

Albert looked back. The man's eyes were like little black plastic buttons.

"How much to look?" Reo Bascom asked Albert.

"Nobody looks," Albert said.

"Only the owner," Wendell said.

"Okay, how much to own it?" Reo Bascom asked.

Albert could tell that Reo Bascom was itchy to have it.

"I can't imagine the circumstances under which I'd part with it," Wendell said. "If I ever change my mind, I'll let you know."

"Sure," Reo Bascom said. "Great. Who cares? How about lunch tomorrow? Just you and me. We'll talk over old times."

"Nothing like old times," Wendell said.

"Here," Reo Bascom said. "One-thirty."

"I'm already looking forward to it," Wendell said.

Albert watched Reo Bascom return to his table, where he joined a young woman in a gold dress and a young man who looked like a professional wrestler.

"Some people never change," Wendell said.

"He offered you two thousand dollars to look in your violin case," Albert said.

"He'd have kept going higher if I'd encouraged him," Wendell said. "He's got plenty of money."

"He's the wizard of nosy, isn't he?" Albert said. "He's who we were coming to see all along."

"You're a quick study, Albert," Wendell said. "I'm proud of you."

"Why didn't you let him look?" Albert asked. "Two thousand dollars is a lot of money." It was more than Albert had ever bothered to contemplate.

"It's just the beginning," Wendell said.

Gloria brought Albert's first shrimp cocktail and Wendell's oysters and a basket of warm, crusty rolls.

"Everything to your satisfaction?" she asked.

"Everything is excellent," Albert said, his gaze fixed on the dozen plump shrimp that sat on the mound of ice in the glass bowl.

"If things were any better," Wendell said, picking up an oyster, "we'd probably get arrested."

EIGHT BALL

"I forgot to call my mother!" Albert's voice rang with panic.

"Three ball in the side pocket," Wendell said.

"She's going to kill me," Albert said.

Wendell sank the three ball.

"Call her on this," he said. He handed Albert the cell phone. He lined up his next shot. They were playing pool in the entertainment room of their suite. Hollywood was resting on Albert's shoulder.

"I'll have to call her at work," Albert said.

"Don't forget the area code," Wendell said.

Albert punched in the numbers. "She's definitely going to kill me."

"I'll talk to her," Wendell said.

"I can do it," Albert said.

It rang seven times before Frank the bartender answered.

"Goat Herder Lounge," Frank shouted above the noise. "This is Frank."

"This is Albert," Albert shouted back. "I have to talk to my mother."

"You'd better have a good excuse," Frank said. "She's steamed."

"I'm in for it," Albert said to Wendell as Frank hollered his mother's name.

"Consider it a character-building experience," Wendell said. "Five ball in the corner." He pointed with his cue stick.

Albert heard his mother pick up the phone. "Don't be mad," he yelled before she could say anything.

"Who is this?" Elly asked.

"It's me," Albert said. He could hear the chilliness in her voice.

"Me who?" she asked.

"Me, your son, Albert," he said. "That's who."

"Oh, that me," she said.

"I forgot," he said. "I didn't mean to. I'm sorry."

"So it wasn't your fault?"

"It was my fault. I was having a good time."

"That's your excuse? You were having a good time?"

"You told me to have a good time."

"You should have called me hours ago," Elly yelled. "Of course I'm mad. I almost called the police a dozen times. Are you all right?"

"I'm all right," Albert said. "I'm really sorry. We had dinner at this restaurant called Crombie's. I had three shrimp cocktails and gelato for dessert. That's Italian ice cream. I had three scoops of chocolate. One for each shrimp cocktail. Then we went for a ride on the ferry. The city looked like a million Christmas trees with all the lights turned on."

He decided not to tell his mother about the hotel and the clothes and the limousine and Wendell's friends and Reo Bascom. He'd tell her someday. When he was older. Much older. Maybe.

"Is Wendell behaving himself?" Elly asked. "No monkey business?"

"No monkey business," Albert said.

"You're really having a good time?"

"I am. Are you?"

"I decided to look for a new job."

"What kind of job?"

"Something that puts us on the same schedule," she said. "I'll get the Sunday paper and check the ads."

"How are your feet?"

"Numb," she said. "I have to go. It's busy. What's the number there?"

"She wants to know the phone number," Albert said to Wendell.

"It's taped on the back," Wendell said.

Albert recited it for his mother.

"Tell her hello," Wendell said. "Tell her to stop worrying."

"Wendell says hello," Albert said. "He says to stop worrying."

"I'll stop worrying when I see you," she said. "Call me tomorrow."

"I will," Albert said.

"Don't make me wait so long."

"I won't."

"Don't disappear."

"What?"

"Don't disappear on me, Albert." She hung up.

What did she mean? Why would he disappear? He watched his grandfather sink another ball. Wendell had disappeared on her, maybe she thought he might do the same. Maybe it was something he'd inherited from Wendell.

"She upset?" Wendell asked.

"Yeah," Albert said, "but she was too busy to ask a lot of questions."

"Timing is everything," Wendell said. He missed his shot.

Albert put Hollywood down on the edge of the pool table. "Don't move," he said. The dog stayed put.

"Eleven in the side pocket," Albert said. He moved the stool into position, climbed up on it, and sank his shot. He sank the nine ball, then the ten, then the twelve. Which was the last of the stripes. He took measure of the eight.

"In the corner," he said. He hit the cue ball gently, and it kissed up against the eight, which plopped into the appointed pocket.

"Where'd you learn to do that?" Wendell asked.

"The place my mother worked before the place she works now had a pool table," Albert said.

"Life is full of surprises," Wendell said.

"Tell me about it," Albert said, yawning.

12

SNEAK ATTACK

Hollywood hobbled, skipped, darted, bobbed, weaved, and jumped up and down like an out-of-control pogo stick. Every two seconds he looked back to make sure Albert was still there. Walking Hollywood was a form of entertainment. He sniffed at everything. With his usual serious expression, he peed everywhere, a drop at a time. He was like a hummingbird on three legs.

Albert and Wendell strolled a few feet behind, enjoying the Sunday morning sun. They wore tan linen suits, light blue shirts, yellow neckties, chocolate brown pocket handkerchiefs, and dark glasses.

Carmen followed them in the limousine.

"Amazing," Wendell said.

"What's amazing?" Albert asked.

"This very moment," Wendell said.

"Why?" Albert asked.

"Because we're alive, Albert. Because we're here and the sun is shining and we're not starving or sick or being shot at. Because we're not taken away secretly in the night. Because nobody is stealing our birthright. Because we're dressed like this and walking a three-legged dog, with a limousine chaser. Such moments in time occur rarely. They are to be savored. They don't last long."

Hollywood wanted to be picked up. Albert put him in his pocket. The dog stuck his head out.

"Where to?" Albert asked.

"Let's see where the day takes us," Wendell replied.

They walked the length of Pike Place Market, inspecting its crafts and photographs and figurines made from Mount St. Helens ash and T-shirts and all the stalls filled with flowers and fish and produce.

"I want my six dollars now," Albert said. "I want to buy something for my mother."

Wendell handed him a twenty-dollar bill.

"You'll get your six dollars back later," he said.

"Then why are you giving me twenty?"

"The six dollars you gave me," Wendell said, "is your

investment in the weekend. It's what makes us partners. The twenty is a gift."

"Why?" Albert asked.

"Patience pays dividends," Wendell said.

After Albert bought his mother's presents, Wendell bought him a bag of freshly fried miniature sugar doughnuts that were only just cool enough to eat.

"It's two hours since Willie Two brought us breakfast," Wendell said. "You must be hungry."

"I'm always hungry," Albert said. He broke off a small piece of doughnut and fed it to Hollywood.

Wendell showed Albert the art museum and concert hall. Carmen drove them to the locks that connected Seattle's inland freshwater with the salt water of Puget Sound. As Wendell explained how water locks worked, they watched a ship glide into the large lock and tie up. The bells rang. The gates closed. The lock flooded with water, lifting the ship until it was level with the canal that led to its berth in Lake Union.

Carmen drove them to the one-railed train.

"It's called a monorail," Wendell said. "We'll take it to the Space Needle."

"I'll meet you there," Carmen said.

Albert looked out at the city as they whooshed up Fifth Avenue above the traffic. He wondered what it would be like to ride the monorail every day. Or go to the market for sugar doughnuts. Or eat shrimp cock-tails until they came out his ears.

He saw a multicolored cartoon of a building up ahead. They rode right through it into the station.

The glass-doored elevator zoomed toward the sky. Albert could see the city getting smaller and smaller as they rose, until everything below seemed the size of a child's construction toy.

They circled the observation deck. Albert saw white-topped mountain peaks and water everywhere and a ship being nudged into its dock by a tug. He watched Carmen's limousine pull to a stop in front of the build-ing far below. A seaplane lifted itself slowly from Lake Union.

"Albert?"

"What?" He looked up at his grandfather.

Wendell's complexion was pasty. His forehead was beaded with sweat. He had a hand clamped to his chest.

"Get the phone out of my pocket," Wendell said be-tween clenched teeth. "Call 911."

13

E.R.

The paramedics brought Wendell down the elevator strapped to a gurney. Albert held his grandfather's hand.

"You have the Stradivarius?" Wendell asked.

"I have it," Albert said. Hollywood was in his pocket.

"Let me see," Wendell said.

Albert held it up.

"Don't let it out of your sight," Wendell said. "Don't let anybody look inside."

"I won't," Albert said. He clutched it tightly.

The elevator door opened and Wendell was hurried through the crowd to the ambulance.

"What happened!" Carmen asked as she came up behind Albert.

"He thinks he had a heart attack," Albert said. His voice sounded like it belonged to somebody else. Somebody who was frightened.

"What hospital are they taking him to?" Carmen asked.

"St. Vincent's," Wendell yelled with a sudden burst of strength. "I'm only going to St. Vincent's."

"St. Vincent's it is," the paramedic pushing him said.

"Take care of him," Carmen said to Albert. She headed for the limousine.

Albert watched the paramedics slide Wendell into the back of the ambulance. Hollywood stuck his head out to see what was going on.

"It's all right," Albert said. The dog disappeared.

"My grandson comes with me," Wendell yelled. "I'm not going anywhere without my grandson."

"Hop in," the paramedic said to Albert.

Albert climbed in. The door was shut. The paramedic hooked Wendell up to a machine that showed his heartbeats as a jagged, jumping line on a screen. Ten seconds later, siren blaring, lights flashing, they were under way.

Albert heard the driver on the radio telling the emergency room they were coming.

"Can you chew these?" the paramedic asked Wendell. "They're aspirin."

"Let me have them," Wendell said.

"Is he going to be all right?" Albert asked.

"I'm going to be fine," Wendell said.

"When did the pain start?" the paramedic asked.

"About a half hour ago," Wendell said.

"Is it a sharp pain, or does it feel like pressure?"

"I feel like I got a hippopotamus on my chest," Wendell said.

Albert laughed. "I'm sorry," he said.

"You were supposed to laugh," Wendell said.

"Any history of heartburn or acid reflux?" the paramedic asked.

"Garlic is a killer," Wendell said. "Otherwise, no problems."

"Are you dizzy?"

"Light-headed," Wendell said.

"This will help." The paramedic put a mask over Wendell's nose and mouth. "Oxygen," he said to Albert.

Albert felt Hollywood stirring in his pocket. He petted him. He watched his grandfather carefully. Wendell looked like the life had drained out of him.

"Don't die," Albert said.

Wendell pulled off the oxygen mask. "I wouldn't dream of it. You still have the Stradivarius?"

"Right here," Albert said. He held it up.

"Why don't you take it easy, Mr. Healy," the paramedic said, putting the mask back in place. "We'll have you there in a minute."

Albert leaned in close to his grandfather. "Who's Mr. Healy?" he whispered.

"I am," Wendell whispered back. "And you're Albert Healy. Until I'm out of the hospital."

The driver hit the "GETOUTOFTHEWAY!" horn as they approached a traffic light. Albert felt them slow, then speed forward as they lurched from side to side.

Albert squeezed Wendell's hand.

Wendell squeezed Albert's.

The ambulance pulled up in front of the emergency room. When the back door flew open, Albert jumped out. The paramedics rushed Wendell inside.

Albert followed them to a white room that was filled with machines. A nurse's aide helped Wendell out of his clothes and into a hospital gown. A nurse hooked him up to a bank of monitors. A doctor breezed in and examined him.

"Who's your regular doctor?" the doctor asked.

"Doc Ringling," Wendell said. "We're from Parson, Montana. He's off fishing. He'll be back a week from tomorrow."

"We're going to want an EKG, Mr. Healy," the doctor

said. "And some of your blood. You'll spend the night so we can keep an eye on you."

The doctor turned to Albert. "We're going to do some tests on your grandfather," he said, saying each word slowly as though he was trying to explain something to an idiot. "We're going to keep him overnight. Do you have somewhere to stay?"

"I do," Albert said. He'd stay at the hotel.

"We have friends here," Wendell said. "He'll call the rest of the family. My grandson's a smart boy."

"Try to relax, Mr. Healy," the doctor said. "We'll be in touch with Dr. Ringling's replacement and check your history. I'll be back."

"Who do you want me to call?" Albert asked.

"Nobody," Wendell said. "Especially not your mother. Not a word to Elly."

"Mr. Healy?" A short, round black man with a British accent walked into the room. He was carrying a clipboard. "I'm Harry. I have a few questions."

"Shoot," Wendell said.

"Your present address?"

"Nine Billups Road, Parson, Montana." Wendell said. He provided a zip code, phone number, and other information, none of which was true.

"Do you have insurance, Mr. Healy?"

"I do," Wendell said. "I'm covered by the International Brotherhood of Assayers and Diviners. My grandson will bring you the card first thing in the morning. It has all the information on it."

"First thing?" Harry asked. "Very first thing?"

"First thing," Albert said.

"That card is important," Harry said.

"I'll have it here," Albert said.

"I'll make sure of it," Wendell said.

"What's the International Brotherhood of Assayers and Diviners?" Albert asked when they were alone again.

"We're a group that knows where to find it and knows what it's worth," Wendell said.

"Find what?" Albert asked.

"Opportunity," Wendell said.

"What are we going to do in the morning when they find out that we're not the Healys and that there's no card?"

"We're not going to be here in the morning," Wendell said.

14

TO FLEE OR NOT TO FLEE

Wendell sat up and reached to start unhooking himself from the various machines.

"What are you doing?" Albert asked. "The doctor said you had to stay overnight."

Wendell, his hand poised on the first wire, stopped to look at his grandson.

"He said so," Albert said.

"He's wrong," Wendell said.

"You're sick," Albert said.

"I had an episode," Wendell said. "It's over. There's nothing they can do for me here."

"They want to do tests."

"They'll do all their tests and they won't find anything and they'll charge me ten thousand dollars I don't have."

"You had a heart attack."

"An episode, Albert. An episode."

"It would be better to stay until tomorrow," Albert said. "You don't look so good."

"Tomorrow is a day too late," Wendell said. "Give me a hand getting these wires off." He reached again for the first of them.

"Why is tomorrow a day too late?" Albert asked.

"Because it is," Wendell said. "Get me my clothes."

"Why?" Albert demanded.

Wendell lay back on the bed, like he didn't have the strength to go on. "I'm going to need your help, Albert. This has kind of knocked me out. Can you keep a secret?"

"If I have to."

"You have to."

"Then I will."

"Reo Bascom is the man who got me sent to jail," Wendell said. "He doesn't know I know it. I'm going to teach him a lesson. We are. You and me. We're going to con a con man. There's nothing sweeter, trust me."

"How are we going to con a con man?" Albert asked.

"In my shoe," Wendell said, "there's a key."

Albert found it.

"It unlocks the violin case," Wendell said.

Albert laid the case on the bed and inserted the key into the lock.

"Turn it to the left," Wendell said.

Albert unlocked the case, then stepped back, as though he was afraid to look.

"You're the first person other than me to open it," Wendell said.

"You sure it's okay?"

"It's okay if I say it's okay," Wendell said.

Albert put his hands on the case, then withdrew them.

"If we're going to be partners," Wendell said, "you have to know what I know. You have to know every-thing."

Still Albert hesitated.

"Reo Bascom deserves what he gets," Wendell said. "He hurts people who can't afford it. He takes advan-tage of the old and the young. He needs a lesson in hu-mility."

"What do I have to do?" Albert asked.

"Nothing illegal," Wendell said. "Nothing that will get you into trouble. Go ahead. Open it."

Albert lifted the lid of the case. He peered inside for a long moment, then closed the case and locked it. He held out the key to his grandfather.

"I don't understand," Albert said.

"You will," Wendell said. "Put the key in my shoe."

A nurse wheeled a cart into the room. "You have a little extra blood for us, Mr. Healy?"

Albert stuck the key in his pocket and snatched the case off the bed.

The nurse drew blood quickly and painlessly. "You have good veins, Mr. Healy."

"My blood is like fine wine," Wendell said. "It improves with age."

The nurse laughed. She was charmed by Wendell, by his interest in what she was doing, by his interest in her.

"The doctor will be in to see you soon, Mr. Healy," she said.

"We'd better get a move on," Wendell said when she was gone. "You have a lunch date with Reo Bascom in forty-five minutes."

15
THREE TO GET READY

Wendell told Albert the plan. After making a few phone calls, he quickly freed himself from the machines and got dressed.

"Hurry," he said to Albert. "They'll be coming to see why the machines aren't working."

Albert looked up and down the hall. He waved Wendell out of the room. He saw the doctor who'd examined his grandfather and waved Wendell back.

"Pulling those wires sets off alarms," Wendell said.

They heard a commotion starting to build at the nurses' station.

"All clear," Albert whispered.

Wendell followed Albert to the reception area.

"Wait here," Albert said. He approached the admitting clerk.

"I'm looking for my grandfather," Albert said. "His name is Healy. He's supposed to be in here."

"Healy?"

"Healy."

As the clerk started to swing in his chair to the computer, Hollywood stuck his head out. The clerk swiveled back.

Hollywood dove into Albert's pocket.

"You can't bring a dog in here," the clerk said.

"What dog?" Albert asked.

"I saw a dog," the clerk said.

"No you didn't," Albert said. He held his arms in the air. He opened his jacket. A little.

"No dog," he said.

"I saw a dog."

"Maybe it was a reflection," Albert said.

The clerk studied Albert, deciding what to do. "Healy," he said finally. "I'll take a look."

Wendell snuck past while the clerk was bent over his computer.

The limousine was waiting outside. Carmen opened the door, and Wendell and Albert got in. Willie Two, Hugo, and a nurse dressed in white greeted them.

"Good to see you, Wendell," the nurse said, taking a blood pressure cuff from her kit.

"Good to see you, Agnes," Wendell said. He sat next to her.

"How you feeling?" Willie Two asked.

"Better than an hour ago," Wendell said. "Let's get going."

An ambulance pulled in as the limousine pulled out. Agnes took Wendell's blood pressure.

"And how are you doing?" Hugo asked Albert.

"I don't know," Albert said. He took Hollywood from his pocket and put him on his lap.

"You should have seen him in there," Wendell said. "Calm, cool, and collected. Professional all the way."

He turned to his grandson. "You're okay about doing this? I don't want to involve you in something you're against."

"It's for a good reason," Albert said.

"You got that right," Willie Two said.

"Reo Bascom has cheated all of us at one time or another," Hugo said.

"Including me and my father," Carmen said.

"How's my blood pressure?" Wendell asked.

"I've seen better," Agnes said. She took his pulse.

"I've gone over it with Albert," Wendell said. "He knows what he has to do."

"I'll make sure he gets there and back," Carmen said.

"What's to keep Reo Bascom from grabbing the Stradivarius and running?" Albert asked. "I'm a kid. I can't stop him."

"I'll be there," Hugo said. "Gloria will be waiting on your table."

"I'll be sitting nearby," Willie Two said. "Where he can't see me. He tries anything, I'll be all over him."

"I'll be outside," Carmen said. "He comes out the door with the Stradivarius, I'll run him over."

"Nothing to worry about," Wendell said. "You'll be well looked after."

"Anyway," Albert said, "Hollywood will bite him if he gets too close."

Hollywood looked up and growled.

"I need the key," Wendell said. "You have to be able to tell him I have it with absolute conviction. That's what sets up the next meeting."

Albert took the key from his pocket and handed it to his grandfather.

"This is a great day," Wendell said, putting an arm around Albert's shoulder.

The limousine glided to a stop by the delivery entrance to the hotel. Willie Two lifted a wheelchair from the trunk and unfolded it.

"I'll check in by phone," Willie Two said.

"So will I," Hugo said.

"Ditto," Carmen said.

Wendell sat in the wheelchair and looked up at Albert.

"I hope I don't make any mistakes," Albert said.

"You'll be great," Wendell said.

"Piece of cake," Albert said.

"Now you're talking," Wendell said.

Albert watched Agnes wheel his grandfather into the back entrance of the hotel.

"Better let Hollywood do his business," Albert said. He set the dog down. Hollywood peed on one of the limousine's tires.

Albert picked him up and climbed into the back with Willie Two and Hugo.

"Let's go," Albert said.

16

THE KEY

"Stop at the corner," Hugo said. "I'll take Willie Two through the kitchen."

"All set?" Willie Two asked Albert.

"I am," Albert said.

"Give it a minute before you come in," Hugo said.

Albert nodded.

Willie Two and Hugo got out, and Carmen drove the limousine slowly up the block to Crombie's. Three orange rubber cones blocked the street in front of the restaurant. Carmen moved them, then parked.

"How you feeling?" she asked.

"I'm a little nervous," Albert replied.

"There'd be something wrong with you if you weren't," she said.

"Well, there's nothing wrong with me then," he said.

"You're an actor playing a part," she said. "Think of it like that."

"Is Wendell going to be okay?" he asked.

"I don't think you have to worry about that."

"Has he had this before?"

"People get old, Albert. Things happen. My father had a heart attack. He's still kicking."

"How old is he?"

"Older than Wendell."

"What's he do?"

"He's retired. It's time."

Albert put Hollywood in his pocket. "Anybody tries anything, let them have it," he whispered to the dog.

Hollywood growled a low growl to let Albert know he was ready for action.

Carmen opened the door, and Albert stepped out carrying the violin case.

"Break a leg," she said.

"Why would I do that?" Albert asked.

"It's show business for kick butt," she said.

"Thank you," Albert said. He walked inside.

"Right this way," Hugo said, leading him to the banquette where he and Wendell had had dinner the night before. Reo Bascom and the wrestler were waiting.

"My grandfather had an episode," Albert said. "They took him to the emergency room at St. Vincent's hospital. Now he's at the hotel with the nurse. He has to rest."

Albert sat down.

Reo Bascom eyed the violin case. "How come you have the Stradivarius?"

"Wendell gave it to me," Albert said. "It's mine now."

"Take a walk," Reo Bascom said to the wrestler. "The young gentleman and I have business to discuss."

The wrestler left without a word. The man's arms nearly reached the floor. He could be in a zoo, Albert thought.

Reo Bascom's gaze stayed fixed on the violin case. "How is the Stradivarius today?"

"As ever," Albert said. "As always."

"Why'd he give it to you?"

"It's my legacy."

"Yeah, but why you?"

"I'm his grandson," Albert said.

"What are you going to do with it?" Reo Bascom asked.

Gloria appeared. "Good to see you, Mr. Bascom," she said. She smiled at Albert. "What can I bring you?"

"Pink lemonade," Albert said. "Please."

Reo Bascom ordered a glass of draft beer.

"Have you decided on lunch?" Gloria asked.

"Shrimp cocktail," Albert said.

Reo Bascom ordered crab cakes.

"What kind of episode did Wendell have?" Reo Bascom asked.

"A heart episode," Albert said. "I don't know how serious it was. They wouldn't tell me. I'm a kid. Grownups don't tell kids much."

"I'm sorry," Reo Bascom said.

Albert looked straight into Reo Bascom's face. Nothing in it indicated that Reo Bascom ever felt sorry about anything.

"I'll tell him you said so," Albert said.

Reo Bascom shifted himself in the banquette so he was closer to Albert. "Why'd he send you?"

"Wendell wanted you to know that he feels bad about having to miss lunch. He said he was looking forward to talking over old times. He said life is too short."

"Wendell and I did some business together once," Reo Bascom said. "He ever say anything about that?"

"He never said your name to me before last night," Albert said. "He said he was glad to see you."

Gloria brought the drinks. "Your lunch will be right out." She smiled at Albert again.

Albert felt himself smiling back, then growing warm.

"So, how's it feel?" Reo Bascom asked.

Albert looked at him blankly.

"To own the Stradivarius?"

"I don't know," Albert said. "It's only been mine for a couple of hours."

"He gave it to you after the episode?"

"In the hospital," Albert said. "He said he wanted me to have it before he died so I might as well have it now."

"Ever wonder what's inside?"

"The Stradivarius," Albert said. "That's what Wendell says."

"I know what Wendell says," Reo Bascom said. "Everybody knows what Wendell says. The big question is, what is the Stradivarius?"

"It's a violin made by the Stradivari family in the 1600s or 1700s," Albert said. "They're the best violins in the world."

"You really think there's a violin in there?" Reo Bascom asked.

"I asked Wendell if he played the violin and he said no," Albert said.

"Aren't you curious?" Reo Bascom asked. "I am. You

don't carry your lunch in a violin case like this one. The case is expensive, Albert. Something expensive on the outside usually has something expensive on the inside. Something of substantial value. Why don't we take a look together?"

Reo Bascom moved closer.

Gloria set Reo Bascom's crab cakes in front of him. She winked at Albert when she set his shrimp cocktail down.

Albert knew that Willie Two was watching them through the leaves of a potted plant. And that Carmen was watching through the restaurant's big front window with her opera glasses. He felt safe but not completely safe.

"The thousand dollars I said I'd give Wendell," Reo Bascam said, "I'll give to you."

"You told Wendell two thousand," Albert said.

"Two thousand, then," Reo Bascom said. "You ever see that much money?"

"I saw a hundred-dollar bill once," Albert said.

"I'm talking about twenty new, crisp, never-been-used-before one-hundred-dollar bills," Reo Bascom said. "Imagine what you could do with all that money."

"I don't think I can imagine it," Albert said.

"It's your legacy, Albert," Reo Bascom said. "You can imagine anything you want."

"I don't have the key," Albert said. "Wendell said he'd give it to me later."

"Why'd he give you the case without the key?" Reo Bascom asked. "What kind of legacy is that? I thought you said it was yours."

"It is mine," Albert said. "Wendell said it was a big responsibility to have the Stradivarius. He wants me to get used to it. He said he'd give me the key when I asked for it."

"So ask for it," Reo Bascom said, unmasking his growing impatience with the boy.

"I will when I'm ready," Albert said.

Reo Bascom reached for the violin case.

Albert pulled it away.

Reo Bascom reached for Albert.

Hollywood rose up out of Albert's pocket and snapped his sharp needles of teeth at Reo Bascom's hand.

Reo Bascom yanked his hand away.

Hollywood disappeared inside Albert's jacket.

"What was that?" Reo Bascom inspected his hand to make sure it was still there.

"My killer dog," Albert said. "He was trained in the army."

Hugo showed up at the table with a big smile. "Everything to your satisfaction, Mr. Bascom?"

"Yeah, fine," Reo Bascom said. "We're busy here, Hugo. Beat it." He took a bite of a crab cake.

"Things couldn't be better," Albert said. That was the code to pass on to Wendell that things were going as predicted. He bit a shrimp in half.

Reo Bascom finished chewing his crab cake. He chewed slowly, like he was making up his mind about something important. He sipped at his beer. He wiped his mouth with his napkin. He brought his focus to Albert.

"So, what are you going to do with the Stradivarius?" he asked.

Albert shrugged his shoulders. He ate another shrimp. He saw Gloria watching them.

"What if I offered to buy it?" Reo Bascom said. "What if I paid you enough so you could do whatever you want?"

"I want to go to college," Albert said.

"How much is that?"

"I don't know," Albert said, "but that's what I want to do. I want to go to college."

Reo Bascom leaned in as close to Albert as he could get without alarming Hollywood. "I could just take it, you know. I could break the lock. I could look inside for nothing. That stupid little dog isn't going to stop me."

"Yes he is," Albert said. "Besides, if you break the lock, the case won't be worth so much. In addition to which, I'll yell. Also, Wendell will come after you."

Reo Bascom pulled back. "You're a smart kid. How are we going to do this?"

"Wendell said he wanted you to come see him at the hotel this afternoon. He wants you to have a drink. He can't have one because of his episode. He wants to talk about the good old days. If I tell him I want to sell the Stradivarius to you because I want to go to college, he'll have to say it's okay."

"What time this afternoon?" Reo Bascom asked.

"Five o'clock," Albert said. "The Palace. Come to the loading dock. Wendell doesn't want anyone knowing he's got visitors."

Albert got up and walked out, the violin case clutched to his side, just the way his grandfather had instructed him to.

Willie Two delivered Albert to Wendell, who was waiting by the door in his wheelchair, a blanket tucked
around his lap.

"Everything went aces," Willie Two said.

"Thank you, Willie Two," Wendell said.

"All for one, one for all," Willie Two said. "I'll check
in later."

Nurse Agnes wheeled Wendell into the living room.
Albert put Hollywood on the floor, and the dog
bounded about, then jumped up on the couch. Wendell
looked old again, Albert thought. He looked frail.

"How are you feeling?" Albert asked.

"Terrific, now that you're back," Wendell said.

"You don't look terrific," Albert said.

"Looks can be deceiving," Wendell said. "I want to know about lunch. I want to hear every word Reo Bascom said. Details, Albert. I want details."

Albert repeated every word he could recall. He answered every question. Wendell was more than satisfied.

"An outstanding performance, Albert," he said. "Absolutely outstanding."

"I don't like Reo Bascom," Albert said.

"What's to like?" Wendell said.

"He's mean. I can tell."

"He's a hollow man," Wendell said.

"Why does he want to buy what's inside the case if he doesn't know what's in it?" Albert asked.

"Because he can't stand not having it," Wendell said. "That's how the mind works. People want what they can't have."

"What do we do now?" Albert asked.

"I don't know about you," Wendell said, "but I'm taking a nap."

"Can I use the cell phone?"

"Tell her hello," Wendell said, handing it over. "If she asks, I'm having the time of my life. If she asks . . . Well, I'll leave it to you."

Hollywood followed Albert to their bedroom. Albert picked him up and petted him. He realized how frightened he'd been in Reo Bascom's presence. But it had also been exciting. He'd accomplished his mission.

His thoughts shifted to the prospect of living on the road with Wendell. They could be permanent partners. His grandfather could teach him. It was in his genes. It was something he could do with his life. Then he thought about his mother and called home.

"Ow!" Elly yelled as she pulled the receiver from its cradle. "Sorry. Hello?"

"What happened?" Albert asked. "Are you all right?"

"I'm making hard-boiled eggs for egg salad," Elly said. "I guess I put too much water in the pot and some of it bubbled over and spritzed on my hand."

"Run cold water on it."

"Yes, doctor. I'm doing it right now. What have you been up to today?"

"Wendell took me to Pike Place Market," Albert said. "We went to the locks and watched a ship come in. We took a ride on the monorail and went to the top of the Space Needle. I had shrimp cocktail for lunch. Wendell's taking a nap." It all came out like a big rush of wind.

Elly laughed.

Albert laughed.

"How is Wendell?" she asked.

"He says he's having the time of his life," Albert said. "So am I."

"Is he behaving himself?" she asked.

"No monkey business," Albert said.

"Maybe he is finally slowing down," she said.

"He's been moving pretty slow," Albert said.

"I'm glad you're having a good time," she said.

"I like it here," Albert said. "There's a lot going on. I like the noise. There are seagulls flying all around the city. Wendell says you can see eagles sometimes. He says that not far away you can see whales."

"We're going to take a vacation," she said. "The first minute we can. We're going to see some things and have a good time. Where do you want to go?"

"Someplace we've never been," he said. He wasn't coming back to Seattle for a long time. Not after doing business with Reo Bascom.

"We could go to Hawaii and take surfing lessons," she said.

"We could go to Alaska and see the aurora borealis," Albert said.

"We'll go to the library and get some books," she said. "We'll pick a place together."

"I've been thinking," Albert said.

"Me too," Elly said. "We're going to work out a new situation for ourselves."

"I'm going to do better in school."

"We're both going to get squared away."

"I'm going to pay attention."

"I saw a couple of ads for jobs in the paper this morning. I looked at ads for apartments in Boise."

"We're moving to Boise?"

"It's a possibility," she said. "Would that be okay?"

"That would be great," Albert said. But maybe he wouldn't be around to move to Boise, he thought. Maybe he'd be on the run with Wendell. For a fleeting moment he thought to tell his mother what was going on with him and Wendell and Reo Bascom. She'd be mad, then disappointed, which was worse. The whole thing with Reo Bascom would have to be called off. He'd have to go home right away. That wouldn't be fair to Wendell. His grandfather had a right to even the score.

"We'll have to get lucky," Elly said. "I'll have to find a better job than I have."

"I feel lucky," he said. "I feel like something good is going to happen soon."

"So do I," she said. "For starters, you'll be back tomorrow. It's hard to imagine anything better than that."

"How soon can we move to Boise?"

"As soon as possible. That soon enough?"

"The sooner the better," he said.

Hollywood barked at a seagull that was perched outside the window.

"What was that?" Elly asked.

The seagull flew away.

"Somebody's dog," Albert said. "Barking at a bird." It occurred to him that tomorrow he'd have to give Hollywood back to Big Royal.

"Maybe we could get a dog," he said.

"There's no room here for a dog," she said.

"A small one."

"If we're moving to Boise it could be a problem."

"Really small."

"Most apartments don't take pets."

"I understand," Albert said. "No dog. Unless we get lucky."

"If we get lucky," she said, "anything is possible."

She talked about how hot it was in Mountain View and about how nice it must be near the water.

"You can go rafting on the Boise River in summer," she said.

He talked about what you could see from the top of the Space Needle and about going out for another big dinner and getting an early start in the morning to come home.

When they hung up, Albert thought about moving to Boise. It wasn't likely to happen. Tomorrow everything would go back to the way it had been. No matter how much he wished it were otherwise. Unless he didn't go back.

18

THE FIVE-FINGER CONTRACT

Albert watched the red Cadillac convertible pull into the delivery entrance of the hotel at 4:59. He was standing on the loading platform. The wrestler was driving. Reo Bascom slouched in the passenger seat.

"Wendell said just you," Albert said to Reo Bascom. "And the car can't stay there. You have to park it."

Reo Bascom let himself out, waved the wrestler away, and the red Cadillac drove off.

"How come you don't want to carry on with the family business?" Reo Bascom asked as Albert led him to the freight elevator. "What's with college? You can't make any money in college."

"I'm going anyway," Albert said.

The elevator door opened, and a room service waiter pushed a cart out. He eyed Albert and Reo Bascom suspiciously.

Albert flashed his ID badge. "How you doing?" he asked the room service waiter.

The room service waiter grunted and moved on.

"There's a lot happening in the world," Albert said on the ride up. "I want to know about it."

"Like what?" Reo Bascom asked.

"If I knew that," Albert said, "I wouldn't have to go to college."

They made their way down the hall to the presidential suite.

"Everything all set?" Reo Bascom asked.

"I'm going to tell him I want to sell you the Stradivarius," Albert said. "He's going to get real upset about that. Then you're going to talk to him about how much."

"I thought we agreed on a price," Reo Bascom said.

"Whatever it costs to go to college," Albert said.

"What's the dollar figure for that?" Reo Bascom asked. "I need to know the ballpark."

"You have to talk to Wendell," Albert said.

"You aren't trying to con me, are you?" Reo Bascom asked. "That would be a mistake."

"You're the one who wants to buy it," Albert said.

"Something like that," Reo Bascom said, smiling suddenly.

Albert smiled back. "You said you did business with my grandfather before."

"In a manner of speaking," Reo Bascom said.

"Now you can do it again," Albert said. He unlocked the door and led Reo Bascom to the living room. Wendell greeted him from his wheelchair. Nurse Agnes stood in attendance.

"Thanks for coming," Wendell said.

"I wouldn't have missed it," Reo Bascom said, looking around. "Impressive set of rooms."

"I got the weekend rate," Wendell said.

They shared a laugh.

"Money isn't my problem," Wendell said. "It's my health. Money can't fix that. Albert, make Mr. Bascom a gin and tonic. Agnes, if I need you, I'll yell."

Nurse Agnes took her leave.

"Where's the Stradivarius?" Reo Bascom asked.

"In a safe place," Albert said.

"He takes good care of it," Wendell said.

Albert made Reo Bascom a gin and tonic the way Wendell had shown him. He poured Wendell a glass of club soda. He opened a bottle of lemonade.

"You're starting him young," Reo Bascom said, lowering himself into a chair.

"Albert is his own man," Wendell said.

"Good for you, Albert," Reo Bascom said. He tipped his glass in Albert's direction. "To the future."

"I'm looking forward to it," Wendell said.

"It's a nice touch, the two of you dressing the same," Reo Bascom said. "Where do you live, Albert?"

"It's none of your business where he lives," Wendell said. "Or what his last name is, or anything about him. The only reason he's here is because I promised him a weekend."

"You've got a good teacher," Reo Bascom said to Albert.

"He's my grandfather," Albert said. "My teacher is Mrs. Hissendale."

"He's a natural," Wendell said, "but his mother would kill me. I may be sick, but I'm not ready to die."

"What kind of episode did you have?" Reo Bascom asked.

"Nothing serious," Wendell said.

"I called the hospital," Reo Bascom said. "They never heard of you."

"I was not myself in the hospital."

"They did say an old man came in with a heart attack, then checked himself out without telling anybody."

"You could get sick in the hospital," Wendell said.

"Sick enough to give Albert the Stradivarius?" Reo Bascom asked.

"This way he avoids paying inheritance tax," Wendell said.

"I decided to sell the Stradivarius to Mr. Bascom," Albert announced. "I thought about it, and that's what I want to do."

"No!" Wendell shouted with what seemed like genuine shock and anger. "Absolutely not. The Stradivarius is not for sale."

He turned his wrath on Reo Bascom. "I don't know what you told my grandson at lunch, but I'm not letting you pull any fast ones on him."

"You said it was mine!" Albert shouted.

"Not to sell!" Wendell shouted back.

"You gave it to me."

"To keep," Wendell said. "To use someday." He shook his head back and forth, as though he couldn't believe what was happening.

"Did you give it to him or not?" Reo Bascom asked. "I don't want to waste my time here."

"I kept the secret all these years," Wendell said to Albert, "How could you do this to me?"

"I want the money to go to college," Albert said.

"I don't care what you want it for," Wendell said. He started to wheel himself from the room.

Reo Bascom looked back and forth between Albert and Wendell. He seemed amused by the proceedings.

"Why'd you send him to have lunch with me if you don't want to sell it?" Reo Bascom asked.

Wendell stopped wheeling. "To express my regrets at not being able to make it," he said. "To invite you for a drink. I didn't want you to think I was insulting you by canceling."

"You can't con a con man," Reo Bascom said.

"And yet here we are," Wendell said, turning himself around.

"I want to go to college," Albert said. "This is the only chance I'm going to have to get the money."

"You should listen to your grandson, Wendell." Reo Bascom sipped his drink.

"I want to learn something," Albert said. "I want to do something with my life."

"You're sure this is how you want to do it?" Wendell asked.

"I'm sure," Albert said.

"Nobody in our family ever went to college," Wendell said. He wheeled himself to Reo Bascom.

"I'll approve the deal for the price of Harvard University," he said.

"I'm not buying him a school," Reo Bascom said.

"Four years at Harvard," Wendell said.

"What if I don't get into Harvard?" Albert said. "What if I don't want to go there?"

"If you can afford Harvard," Wendell said, "you can afford anywhere. That's six years from now. By then Harvard will cost fifty grand a year."

"That's two hundred thousand dollars," Reo Bascom said.

"The Stradivarius is worth a million," Wendell said.

"It could be worth nothing," Reo Bascom said.

"You won't know until it's yours," Wendell said.

"Maybe I've lost interest," Reo Bascom said. "Maybe I'll pass."

"Good," Wendell said. "I don't want to sell it anyway. And you can forget the good old days." He started wheeling himself away.

Reo Bascom started for the door.

"Then I'll sell it to somebody else," Albert said.

Reo Bascom stopped in his tracks.

Wendell wheeled himself back.

"You said a lot of people want to buy it," Albert said to Wendell. "I'll sell it to one of them."

"You don't know any of those people," Wendell said.

"I'll find them," Albert said. "I'll put it up for sale on the Internet."

"He can sell it if he wants to," Wendell said, spinning around to face Reo Bascom. "But I set the terms.

Four years at Harvard. Two hundred grand. No nego-
tiation. Offer expires in sixty seconds."

"Why not?" Reo Bascom said, like two hundred thousand was pocket change.

"Used bills," Wendell said. "Nothing bigger than a
fifty."

"Just me and Albert," Reo Bascom said. "Nobody
else is around."

"At the park," Wendell said. "By the old water
tower."

"Midnight," Reo Bascom said.

"Four in the morning," Wendell said.

"Albert brings the Stradivarius and the key," Reo
Bascom said. "He gets the cash."

"Straight up," Wendell said. "I'll make sure Albert
understands the procedure."

"I'm sure he won't have any trouble," Reo Bascom
said.

Wendell contemplated his grandson. "You really
want to do this?"

"I do," Albert said.

"I won't say I'm happy," Wendell said. "I'd hoped for
more. But at least it's for a good cause."

He turned to Reo Bascom. "After right now, I never
want to see you again."

Reo Bascom extended his hand to Wendell.

"Your deal is with Albert," Wendell said. He wheeled himself away.

Reo Bascom strode across the room to Albert, his hand out in front of him. "The five-finger contract," he said.

Albert shook it, pulling free as quickly as he could.

"If your grandfather tries anything funny," Reo Bascom said, "you're the one who will pay."

Hollywood popped out of Albert's pocket with a growl.

"Your dog I'll put in a meat grinder," Reo Bascom said. He let himself out.

"I think that went well," Wendell said as he wheeled himself back into the room. "Now you've got to get ready for tonight."

19

SCHOOL

"This isn't the seventh grade, Albert," Wendell said. "This isn't college. This is life. You have to pay attention. You have to remember. You have to be ready for the unexpected."

Albert, Hollywood in his pocket, the violin case in his right hand, stood in the middle of the living room, hanging on every word.

Wendell described the old water tower where Albert was going to meet Reo Bascom. He told him about the trees and the dark places where somebody who wasn't supposed to be there could hide. He took him through the meeting, step by step.

"You have to know where everything is," Wendell said. "You have to be able to get out of there in a hurry."

Albert began to see the place in his mind's eye.

"You don't have to be afraid of Reo Bascom," Wendell said. "He wants the Stradivarius, not you."

"What happens when he finds out what's inside?" Albert asked.

"Well, I wish I could see his face when he finds out," Wendell said. "But sadly you and I will have to miss that happy moment. We'll be gone by then."

"He'll open it right away," Albert said. "While I'm still there."

"I have something that will slow him down a little," Wendell said. He wheeled himself to his grandson.

"He doesn't know where you live," Wendell said. "He doesn't know anything about you. If he comes after anybody, it'll be me."

Wendell touched his grandson's face. "You don't have to do it. I can show up instead."

"Then he'll know something's wrong," Albert said. "He won't do it if it's you. I just want to make sure I get it right."

Wendell started from the top. They covered Albert's arrival and his approach to the water tower. They went over the meeting and the exchange, and what Albert was supposed to do and say, and how he was supposed to get out of there.

Time became a blur to Albert as Wendell put him through the drill again and again. Each step of the operation was choreographed. Every contingency was explored. Wendell confronted Albert with unexpected changes in Reo Bascom's possible behavior.

When Albert thought he could stand it no longer, Willie Two showed up with sandwiches, lemonade, and coffee.

"Everything ready?" Wendell asked.

"All set," Willie Two said.

Five minutes after eating, Albert and Wendell were back at work.

"One more time," Wendell said.

20

THE RIDE

At three-thirty Monday morning, Albert, Hollywood, and Wendell went down to the limousine. Wendell had the Stradivarius in one hand and a cane in the other. Albert carried his backpack and his grandfather's gym bag. Along with Willie Two, they'd tidied up the suite and left it looking like nobody had ever been there. The hallway was filled with painters' gear again.

"And how is Albert Rosegarden today?" Carmen asked, like being up this early was normal.

"Good," he said. But he didn't feel so good. His stomach was upset. He was anxious, and he felt a little fuzzy-headed. He shivered. There was a chill in the air. A breeze was coming in from the bay. He could smell the salt water. They'd spent the night, he and Hollywood, watching the city's lights and listening to trains passing through. He couldn't stop thinking about how extraordinary life could be. He'd fallen asleep finally, an hour before Wendell woke him.

As they drove to the old water tower, Albert tried to imagine what was going to happen when he met Reo Bascom. He was convinced that when the time came, he'd forget everything he was supposed to say and do.

"We should go over it one more time again," he said.

"Better to relax," Wendell said.

"How am I supposed to relax?" Albert asked. He heard Hollywood's low growl and looked down. The dog was looking up at him with what Albert swore was an expression of determination.

"What are you going to do when you get home?" Wendell asked.

"I don't know," Albert said. "Go to school. The usual. What are you going to do?"

"Haven't figured it out yet," Wendell said.

"Where are you going to live?"

"I'll probably keep moving."

"You need an address."

"Don't get any mail."

"What about a phone number?"

"No calls."

"How do people find you?"

"I find them. Like I found you."

"Live with us," Albert said.

"That trailer is a little tight for three people," Wendell said.

"We're moving to Boise," Albert said. "My mother is looking for a new job."

"Your mother wouldn't think much of me moving in," Wendell said.

"We'll talk her into it."

"You think you could do that?"

"We talked her into this trip," Albert said.

"That would be something," Wendell said, "all of us living together. You have any interest in seeing the world?"

"I'd see it if I could," Albert said, "but I don't think there's much chance of that."

"You never know what's going to happen next," Wendell said.

"Are you really retired?" Albert asked.

"Everything changes all the time," Wendell said. "Whether we like it or not."

"We're here," Carmen said.

The limousine entered the park. Carmen turned the headlights off.

"The moment of truth approaches," Wendell said.

"There's not much truth involved in any of this," Albert said.

"It's about as honest as a business transaction gets in this life," Wendell said.

"What's honest about it?"

"Tit for tat," Wendell said. "Eyes wide open. All the players are pros. Except for you. However it turns out, nobody can claim they were taken advantage of."

The limousine made its way along a narrow serpentine road. A quarter moon cast a faint white light across the park's open fields. Rows of thick, gnarled trees stood like sentries at attention.

The limousine stopped.

Albert put Hollywood in his jacket.

Wendell planted a kiss on his grandson's forehead. "You're in charge," he whispered.

Carmen opened the door. Albert clutched the Stradivarius to his side.

"I'll see you," he said.

He watched the limousine drive off. In front of him was the old water tower. Its shingles were rotting. It was covered with moss and ivy. A clump of trees and thick brush grew around it. Leaves rustled. He heard footsteps. Nobody was there. An animal hooted.

Hollywood scratched at Albert with his front paw,

the signal that he had business to attend to. Albert put him down, and the dog peed quickly, as though he knew they didn't have much time. The boy wondered which of them looked more serious.

With Hollywood back in place, Albert started walking toward the spot where he was to meet Reo Bascom.

21

THE EXCHANGE

"Hello, Albert," Reo Bascom said as he stepped out of the shadows. He was dressed in black. He carried a canvas bag.

Albert tightened his grip on the Stradivarius.

"I've got the money," Reo Bascom said.

"I've got the Stradivarius," Albert said.

"And the key?"

"I've got the key."

"Then I guess we'd better get on with it," Reo Bascom said. He took a step toward Albert.

Albert took a step back. "Wendell said to put them on the ground."

"And why would we do that?" Reo Bascom asked. "Are we going to dance a jig?"

"We put them down," Albert said, "then you walk over and get the Stradivarius and key, and I walk over and get the money."

"And why are we doing it that way?" Reo Bascom asked.

"So we don't come near each other," Albert said. "Wendell said we should keep our distance."

"I don't play games, Albert," Reo Bascom said. "Your grandfather should have told you that."

Reo Bascom took another step toward Albert.

Albert took another step back.

"You can't outsmart me, Albert," Reo Bascom said. "Your grandfather tried. He couldn't."

"We do it the way Wendell said, or we don't do it," Albert said. He took another couple of backward steps to show he meant business.

"You should come to work for me," Reo Bascom said. "I could use a boy like you."

"Wendell said if I didn't have the money in three minutes, I should leave," Albert said.

"Wendell can be an irritating man," Reo Bascom said. "You could make a lot of money working for me."

Albert took another step back.

"All right," Reo Bascom said, "we'll do it your way."
He put the bag on the ground.

Albert put the Stradivarius down.

"Where's the key?" Reo Bascom asked.

"Attached to the handle," Albert said.

"I can't see it from here."

"I told you, it's attached to the handle."

"How do I know that?"

"How do I know there's two hundred thousand in the bag?"

"You don't," Reo Bascom said. "Didn't Wendell tell you this is based on trust?"

"It's almost three minutes," Albert said.

"Sure. Whatever you say." Reo Bascom started walking toward the Stradivarius.

Albert started walking toward the canvas bag. He could tell that Reo Bascom was inching toward him. He started inching away.

"Your grandfather is old," Reo Bascom said. "He'll die soon. You could have a long future with me."

They passed within a few feet of each other.

Reo Bascom grabbed Albert.

Hollywood snarled and sank his teeth into Reo Bascom's hand.

Reo Bascom howled and let go.

Albert moved quickly to the canvas bag.

"I'll have you both before this is over," Reo Bascom yelled as he hurried to the Stradivarius.

Albert picked the canvas bag off the ground. It was heavy. Wendell had told him it would be. They'd practiced with a shopping bag filled with newspapers.

"I have the money," Albert said.

"I have the Stradivarius," Reo Bascom said. He examined the case quickly. He found the key attached to the handle. He grinned despite the pain.

Albert walked away.

"Aren't you going to count it?" Reo Bascom asked.

"You said it was all there," Albert said without stopping.

Reo Bascom started freeing the key, which was tied tight to the violin case handle with fishing filament. He couldn't find the knot. His bad hand was useless.

Albert started running.

"You're not going anywhere," Reo Bascom yelled after him. He whistled.

The wrestler came storming out of the trees next to the old water tower.

"Get him!" Reo Bascom screamed. He started biting at the filament.

The wrestler ran after Albert, his stocky body accelerating like a sprinter's.

Albert tried to make his legs move faster, but he

was slowed by the weight of the money. He could hear the wrestler gaining on him.

He heard a motorcycle engine roar to life.

He heard car tires screech behind him.

He left the road and started running across a field.

The wrestler lunged for Albert but missed by a whisker and tumbled hard to the ground.

The motorcycle swooped into view and slid to a stop in the grass. Albert swung the canvas bag to the driver, then jumped on behind and grabbed the driver around the waist, and they raced off.

Albert looked back. He saw Reo Bascom coming after them in the Cadillac convertible.

The motorcycle sped through the pedestrian gate, clearing its stone pillars by inches. It cut a hard right.

Albert held on for dear life. He'd never ridden on a motorcycle before. He thought he was going to fly off any minute. It was like riding his bicycle, only a million times faster.

The Cadillac fishtailed across the road and up onto a lawn as it made the turn after them. Albert could feel the car's headlights on his back.

The motorcycle leapt forward like it had been launched by a rocket. It took Albert's breath away.

The Cadillac honked its horn as it tried to pull even.

The motorcycle weaved its way through a series of side streets, then made another sharp right turn.

Albert glanced over his shoulder. The car was gone.

They cut left, then right, then left again, then made their way through a residential neighborhood. The driver reached back with a gloved hand and patted Albert's leg, a gesture of reassurance. They cut right and headed down a long, steep hill.

Suddenly Albert could see his shadow in headlights again. The Cadillac closed in on them. Albert looked back. He could see Reo Bascom behind the wheel.

The motorcycle cut across the plaza of an office building, then bumped its way down a dozen steps. It straightened out on Third Avenue and headed south.

The car was gone. Albert allowed himself to relax. There was no way it could catch them now.

Then it was there again, bursting out of a side street.

The motorcycle cut right, then left into an alley that was littered with garbage Dumpsters.

The Cadillac turned in after them, skidded, then banged into a Dumpster and stopped. It couldn't get through. Its tires left smoke and the stink of burning rubber as it backed up, then started around the block after them.

The motorcycle cut left on the next street, then left again into a building and down a ramp into a parking garage. The heavy metal door closed behind them.

22

TIME TO SAY GOODBYE

They were all there: Wendell, Hugo, Carmen, Johnny Lark, Eddie the elder, Eddie the younger, Mr. Jay, Willie Two, and Nurse Agnes. They were grinning from ear to ear. When the motorcycle came to a stop, they started applauding.

Gloria turned off the engine, removed her helmet, and hugged Albert.

Hollywood showed his head and barked.

Then Albert was surrounded. His hand was shaken. His back was slapped. The compliments flew fast and furious.

"Time to see what Albert brought us," Wendell said. "Albert, will you do the honors?"

Albert opened the canvas bag and turned it upside down, emptying the contents on the floor. Bundled wads of money fell out, then bundled wads of newspa pers and magazines.

"Reo Bascom cheated us," Albert said. He looked at the others, feeling like he'd let them down.

Wendell took a quick count of the money. "There's a hundred grand here," he said.

"It's supposed to be two hundred," Albert said.

"I knew he'd cut whatever I told him in half," Wendell said, "then try to get it back. That's what his pal in the trees was there for. A hundred was all I was looking for."

He handed out packets of money, the amount according to the role played and the arrangements made. Johnny Lark, Mr. Jay, and the two Eddies were paid for clothes, shoes, and haircuts. They received generous bonuses. Willie Two got twelve thousand. He had people to pay off at the hotel. Carmen, Hugo, and Gloria each received five thousand. Nurse Agnes picked up twenty-five hundred for her services. Wendell gave Gloria an extra thousand for saving Albert's bacon.

Albert wanted to kiss her for saving him. But then, Albert just wanted to kiss her, period.

"Sad to say, Albert," Wendell said, "we have to be on our way."

Wendell put the remaining money in the canvas bag and set it in the camper bus, which was parked next to the limousine.

"It's all gassed up and ready to go," Carmen said.

Albert and Wendell changed into their old clothes inside the camper bus. Albert hardly recognized himself. The suits and all the rest they gave to Johnny Lark to give away.

"What's next?" Willie Two asked.

"The sun is about to rise on a new day," Wendell said. "After that, who knows?"

Wendell said goodbye to everyone. He thanked them all.

Then it was Albert's turn.

"You ever need anything, let me know," Willie Two said.

"I will," Albert said.

"I'll drive you anywhere, anytime," Carmen said. "No charge." She gave him a hug that almost knocked the wind out of him.

"Don't eat too many shrimp cocktails," Hugo said.

"Stay well," Nurse Agnes said.

"Happy feet make a happy body," Mr. Jay said.

"Go to college," Gloria said. She kissed him. "If you were my age . . ." She let the thought die there.

If only I was, Albert thought.

"One last piece of business," Wendell said. He placed the cell phone behind the back tire of the camper bus.

Hollywood took a fast pee on a concrete column.

Albert picked him up and climbed into the camper bus.

Wendell backed over the cell phone, crushing it to smithereens. He raced the engine to get up a head of steam, then released the clutch. They started the slow climb up the ramp.

Albert leaned out the window and waved.

The garage door slid open.

23

THE WAY BACK

The sun appeared in bands of pink and gold above the Cascade Mountains as they headed east. The city was behind them. The weekend was done.

Wendell laughed. "We conned a con man, Albert. We did what can't be done. You're a first-class bamboozler. First-class."

"Bamboozler," Albert said, rolling the word around in his mouth. "We bamboozled him. We're the bamboozlers. We could stay the bamboozlers. I could come with you. I could help. We could do it together."

"I'm never doing it again," Wendell said. "This was the last time. You going to tell your mother about my episode?"

"Are you?"

"Do I look all right?"

"Not too bad," Albert said.

"I feel terrific," Wendell said. "A complete recovery. I don't think I'll bother her with it. She has enough on her mind."

"I'm not telling her if you're not," Albert said. "Could it happen again?"

"Anything can happen," Wendell said. "It's not the things you're looking for that get you. You did a great job, Albert. I couldn't have done it better myself. I couldn't have done it without you."

"See, we could be great together."

"We were great together, Albert. We had a moment of greatness."

Albert tried to put the last couple of days into some sort of perspective. But it seemed more like a dream than something that had actually happened. He wasn't going to get to go with Wendell. Deep down he'd never thought his grandfather would take him. And he couldn't leave his mother. He wouldn't. No matter what. He rested a hand on Hollywood's sleeping body, then dozed off himself.

When he woke up, Wendell handed him a bottle of water.

"Do you think Reo Bascom will come after us?" Albert asked.

"He might if he knew where we were," Wendell said. "But he doesn't. And he's pretty lazy. So I doubt it. He's out the hundred, and there isn't much he can do about it."

"He could sell it to somebody else."

"If he tries," Wendell said, "everybody in the business will know he got stiffed buying Wendell Rosegarden's Stradivarius. His reputation will suffer accordingly."

"Well, I'm not planning on going back to Seattle until a long time from now," Albert said.

"Me neither," Wendell said.

Albert took another drink of water, then handed the bottle back to his grandfather.

"Are you afraid of dying?" he asked.

"Who said I was dying?"

"Reo Bascom said you were old and that you'd die soon."

"One of these days I'll die," Wendell said. "Until then I'll live."

"I'm afraid of a lot of things," Albert said.

"Things like what?" Wendell asked.

"Things like, what's going to happen when I go back to school. Whether my mother will find a new job so we can move to Boise. If we'll be stuck in Mountain View forever. What's going to happen to all of us? Will I ever see you again?"

"That's the whole list?"

"Depends on the day," Albert said.

"That's a heavy load for a boy," Wendell said. "Too much for anybody. Don't worry about what you can't control. Work hard in the areas you can do something about. Don't worry about what hasn't happened yet. It may never come to pass."

"Is that why you don't worry about dying? Because you know you can't do anything about it?"

"I don't worry about dying," Wendell said, "because I don't really exist at all. I don't have a social security number. I don't have any credit cards. I don't have a bank account. I don't have a driver's license." He grinned at Albert.

"Everybody dies," Albert said.

"Sooner or later," Wendell said. "But maybe, since I don't have an address, death won't be able to find me."

"What happens when you die?" Albert asked.

"In my case I want to be cremated," Wendell said.

"That's where they burn your body until all that's left is ashes," Albert said.

"That's it," Wendell said. "Then I want my ashes scattered."

"Where?"

"I'm leaving that up to you. I'll carry a letter that says to contact you when I kick the bucket. You'll take care of things."

"Where do you want them scattered?"

"Not at sea," Wendell said. "I don't care for the water. I wouldn't mind you putting them in a good-looking container, something somebody would like to keep around. Something your mother might put in the house somewhere. On the mantel if you have one. Or in the kitchen."

"She won't do it," Albert said.

"She will when the time comes," Wendell said.

"Is that what happens?" Albert asked. "You die and you end up in a container?"

"I end up what you remember about me," Wendell said. "You'll remember this trip. You'll tell your kids someday. That's what happens when you die. You become part of what's left behind."

They rode for a while in silence. Wendell tried to find some decent music on the radio, then turned it off. The sky was filling with billowy white clouds that looked like ghosts pushing off into the bright blue yonder. They headed south from Ellensburg and passed through Yakima.

"I'm hungry," Albert said.

"Me too," Wendell said. "Hugo packed us something. Right behind you."

Albert turned in his seat and saw the picnic hamper.

"There's a turkey sandwich on top," he said, looking inside.

"I'll take it," Wendell said.

Albert passed it to him, then dug deeper into the hamper. In an insulated container he found six cold shrimp. There was a bottle of pink lemonade.

He fed Hollywood one of the shrimp and ate the rest. He thought about riding on the motorcycle behind Gloria. He tried to imagine what it would be like to be her age.

They finished eating, then were content to ride in silence again. They were at ease in each other's company. Albert thought about his mother. He'd be home in a few hours. They crossed the Columbia River into Oregon.

24

THE LAST LEG

Big Royal was sitting on the porch. A ratty old dog of cloudy lineage was splayed out next to him.

Hollywood hit the ground as soon as Albert opened the camper bus door. He hopped over to Big Royal, barked a greeting, then circumnavigated the ratty old dog, sniffing his way to familiarity. The ratty old dog, who was roughly twenty times Hollywood's size, sneezed.

"Looks like you got yourself a new dog," Wendell said.

"He's called Mister," Big Royal said. "Out of respect for his age."

Mister's muzzle was gray. He'd logged a lot of miles.

"Why'd you get a new dog?" Albert asked.

"I don't like being without one," Big Royal said.

"But you already have a dog," Albert said.

"Hollywood is yours."

"What do you mean, mine?" Albert glanced down at the dog, who was looking up at him.

"He was yours the minute he set eyes on you," Big Royal said. "Don't you want him?"

"Of course I want him," Albert said. "He saved me. We're friends."

"Then it's done," Big Royal said.

"My mother won't let me have a dog," Albert said.

"She'll change her mind when she sees this one," Wendell said.

"You think so?" Albert asked.

"I do," Wendell said.

"You sure it's okay?" Albert asked Big Royal.

"It's destiny," Big Royal said.

Albert hoped they were right. If he showed up with Hollywood, his mother wouldn't have much choice. She wasn't going to put a three-legged dog who fit in a pocket out on the street.

Wendell gave Big Royal a thousand dollars and thanked him for his help.

Albert remembered the letter that was taped to the

inside of the otherwise empty violin case, the one he knew Big Royal had written. He remembered the end of it, word for word.

"Reo Bascom, you own the Stradivarius at last. And now you know that it was never more than a con, the perfect con, the conning of Reo Bascom. By selling him an empty violin case which he couldn't live without. Timing is everything."

Albert understood finally. His grandfather had baited a hook and waited all this time for the fish to bite.

They said goodbye to Big Royal and Mister, then made their slow way, coughing up the long switch-backs of the Blue Mountains.

"I was small-time," Wendell said.

Albert was half asleep.

Hollywood was looking out the window.

"I've spent my life mostly living in motels," Wendell continued. "A square room. A rectangular window. Shag carpets that smell of disinfectant. They're all the same."

The camper bus strained as it neared the summit. They were caught in a line of tractor-trailers.

"I sold things that didn't exist to people who didn't need what I was selling," Wendell went on. "Land that was underwater. Shares of stock in enterprises that existed only in my head. I got people to cash checks on banks that were figments of my imagination. I took advantage of the opportunities I saw. I kept it small on purpose. I've lived a modest life. Nobody ever got hurt. If anybody did, I'm sorry."

The camper bus relaxed as it pointed its front end downhill.

"It's not a life I'd recommend," Wendell said.

A horn honked as a truck passed them. Albert opened his eyes and looked at his grandfather.

"I'm going to take it easy now," Wendell said. "The way I live, that money will last me for the rest of my life."

"I thought the money was for me to go to college," Albert said.

"That was to induce Mr. Bascom into the transaction," Wendell said.

"I want to go to college," Albert said.

"I think that's an excellent idea," Wendell said.

"You did it for yourself," Albert said. "It had nothing to do with me."

"Us doing it together is what it had to do with you," Wendell said. "You and me and the doing of it. That's what matters. I'm old. It's all the money I've got. You'll get to college. I guarantee it."

Wendell reached into his shirt pocket and handed Albert six dollars. "Here's your investment back."

"I thought we were partners," Albert said.

"We were," Wendell said.

"Then shouldn't I get half of what's left?" Albert asked.

"Patience, Albert."

"It's enough money for us to go on the road together," Albert said. "I could help take care of you."

"That's one of the finest offers I've ever had in my life," Wendell said, "but it's better this way."

"It was your Stradivarius," Albert said. "You can do whatever you want." He was angry for a minute, then resigned.

"You had a good time, didn't you?" Wendell asked.

"I did," Albert said.

"It was possibly the most fun I've ever had," Wendell said.

"Me too," Albert said. "I liked eating at Crombie's. I liked it when Hollywood bit Reo Bascom. I liked that a lot. I liked Seattle. I liked all your friends."

"They liked you, Albert."

"You don't have to live in motels," Albert said.

"I'll find something," Wendell said.

"Where?"

"I'll know it when I see it."

"I want you to live with us," Albert said. "We can get a bigger place. You can put something toward the rent. You have your own money so you won't cost anything. We could spend time together when my mother's working."

"Sounds like an idea to me," Wendell said.

"It is an idea," Albert said. This was what he wanted. Not to go on the road but to have his grandfather stay with him.

"I'd like to," Wendell said, "but you know your mother won't go for it."

"She will when I get done," Albert said. Now he had to convince her to let him keep Hollywood and Wendell.

"We could give it our best shot," Wendell said. "How about that?"

"If we can sell Reo Bascom the Stradivarius," Albert said, "we can sell anybody anything."

An hour later they turned up the dirt road to the trailer.

25
ALL'S WELL

When Elly saw Hollywood, she picked him up and he licked her face and that was that. The rest of it came harder.

Albert started to explain why he'd gone off with Wendell without telling her.

"No explanations," she said. "You ever do anything like that again, I'll lock you in your room for the rest of your life."

She turned on Wendell. "Go away," she said. "I never want to see you again."

"You have to let him stay," Albert pleaded.

"No I don't," she yelled. "I won't."

"I like him," Albert said. "He wants to settle somewhere. I want him to live here so I can see him. He has his own money. He won't cost anything."

Elly handed Hollywood to Albert, then marched inside the trailer and slammed the door.

"I don't think she cares for the idea," Wendell said.

"She's thinking it over," Albert said.

"How long will that take?" Wendell asked.

Albert shrugged his shoulders.

A few minutes passed.

"I appreciate what you're trying to do," Wendell said. "I'll let you know when I land somewhere."

"You're landing here," Albert said.

"I'm saying goodbye."

"You're staying until she comes back," Albert said.

"Is that so?" Wendell said.

Albert couldn't tell if his grandfather was amused or annoyed. He didn't care. He tried to send his mother a message from his brain.

Another few minutes passed.

"Albert?"

"What?"

"I think we should say goodbye now."

"No."

The trailer door opened.

"Where's the Stradivarius?" Elly asked. "How come I don't see you carrying it?"

"He left it in Seattle," Albert said. "Somebody else has it now."

"Is that true?" Elly asked her father.

"I'm retired," Wendell said.

"He doesn't need it anymore," Albert said. "Look at him. He's old. Where is he going to go if he doesn't stay with us? We can't send him away. He can sleep in my room. He can help me with my homework. I won't bug you so much."

Elly closed the door.

"We got her," Albert said.

"You think so?" Wendell asked. He sounded skeptical.

"She didn't slam the door that time," Albert said.

Wendell smiled.

The door opened.

"You can stay tonight," Elly said. "If that works out, you can stay tomorrow night. One-day contracts."

"One day's notice is all I require," Wendell said.

"You try teaching Albert any monkey business," she said, "and you're out of here."

"No monkey business," Albert said.

"No monkey business," Wendell said.

"Wendell, this is the only chance you're ever going to get," she said.

"I know," Wendell said. "It means a lot to me that you're giving it."

"I told you it would work out," Albert said. Then he jumped up and down he was so happy. "You can stay," he shouted.

He hugged his grandfather, then ran to his mother and hugged her.

Hollywood licked her face.

"I took the night off," Elly said. "I made dinner." She went inside, scratching Hollywood's chin.

While they downed hot dogs, potato puffs, and coleslaw, Albert answered his mother's questions about the trip. The question she asked most was, "Then what did you do?" She asked it almost every time he got done describing something. In the absence of direct inquiry, he made no reference to Wendell's episode or the conning of Reo Bascom. With his grandfather's help he was able to stretch out the sightseeing and eating to account for their time.

"I almost forgot," Albert said, jumping up and running inside the trailer.

He returned with a T-shirt that had a picture of an umbrella on it and another with a color photograph of Seattle lit up at night.

"I bought them at the Market," he said.

"You didn't have to," Elly said, delighted with her gifts. "I love them both."

They had pound cake with chocolate sauce for dessert. Wendell made coffee. Albert poured himself a glass of milk.

"I answered a couple of ads from the paper," Elly said. "I'm going up to Boise for an interview on Thursday."

"What kind of job?" Albert asked.

"A coffee shop is looking for a manager," she said. "It's mostly days, and it pays more than I'm making now."

"Are you going to get it?" Albert asked.

"They're interested enough to meet me," she said. "We'll see what happens after that."

"She'll get it," Wendell said.

Elly flashed a smile at her father, then realized what she was doing and looked away.

After dinner Wendell showed Albert how to play gin rummy. He showed him how to keep track of his opponent's cards and how to keep score. They played a few hands, then Wendell challenged Elly.

"Come on, daughter," he coaxed. "You know you can't beat me."

She beat him ten straight hands.

"She cheats," Wendell said.

"I play the way you taught me," Elly said.

"I have homework," Albert said. He picked up Hollywood and left the kitchen before his mother could voice her astonishment.

He worked for a while on math and science, then read a chapter in his geography book. He had a lot more to do, but he was tired. This was better than nothing.

He took Hollywood outside to do his business. The dog nosed his way around the trailer until he found what he was looking for. Then he grinned at Albert, as if to say, This new arrangement will do nicely, thank you. Albert grinned back. Then Hollywood got serious and peed.

Albert went to the toilet, washed his face and hands, then brushed his teeth. He said good night to Wendell, who promised to be quiet when he came to bed.

"When I get home from school tomorrow, we'll do something," Albert said.

"Whatever you want," Wendell said.

"I'll show you around Mountain View," Albert said. "You can buy me a piece of pie at Crystal's."

"With ice cream," Wendell said.

Albert kissed his mother. "Thank you," he whispered in her ear.

He laid out his sleeping bag and pillow on the floor of his room and turned out the light. He and Hollywood settled themselves.

"Good night, pal," Albert said.

Hollywood made a small noise in his throat.

The conversation coming from the kitchen sounded like waves lapping up on the beach. It was pleasing to Albert's ear. His mother and grandfather were getting along. Hollywood was already a member of the family. All was well.

26

A GOOD BEGINNING

Albert woke up early. He and Hollywood lay there listening to crowing roosters and whistle blasts from a freight train passing through Mountain View and Wendell's gentle snoring. His grandfather slept peacefully, as though he didn't have a care in the world. How unpredictable life could be, Albert thought. Things went on and on a particular way, then one day they changed and were never the same again. He marveled at how quickly it could happen.

When Albert and Hollywood showed up in the kitchen, Elly was scrambling eggs and frying sausage patties. He thought his mother looked better than she had in a long time. Not so tired. Happier maybe.

"How's it going?" he asked.

"Good," she said. "How's it going with you?"

"Good for me too," he said. "How'd it go last night?"

"He's still here," she said.

"I'm going to take care of school," he said, sitting down to eat. "I know I've said it before, but this time I'll do it."

"I had a whole lecture planned," she said. "You look different. You sound different."

"I was only gone three days," he said.

"Something's definitely different," she said.

"I'm going to take care of business from now on," Albert said. "I won't be getting suspended again. You don't have to worry about that. I decided I want to go to college."

"What made you decide that?"

"I want to know what's going on," he said.

"Okay," she said. "We'll find a way to make that happen. We'll take it like everything else around here."

"One-day contracts," Albert said.

"Renewed daily," she said.

He broke off a piece of sausage patty and fed it to Hollywood.

"He probably should eat dog food," Elly said. "Something healthier than sausage anyway."

"I'm eating sausage," Albert said.

"You should be eating healthier too," she said. "I'm going to start paying more attention to that."

"I'm not eating dog food," Albert said. "I don't care how healthy it is. Anyway, Hollywood's not really a dog. He's a creature from another planet."

Elly sat with her coffee.

"I like having Wendell here," Albert said.

"I know you do," she said. "Your grandfather is a charming man. It's hard not to like him. I don't have much faith that he'll stay."

"I do," Albert said.

"Don't count on him for much," she said. "I don't want you to be disappointed."

"I'm not going to be disappointed," he said, "because there's not going to be anything to be disappointed about."

He wanted to tell his mother how he and Wendell had spent the weekend. He wanted her to know how close they'd gotten. They were a team, Albert and Hollywood and Wendell. Nobody was going anywhere.

He picked Hollywood up so they were face-to-face. "I'm going to take you and Wendell on a tour of Mountain View when I get home, then we're having pie."

"You're going to be late for school," Elly said.

"No, I'm not," Albert said. "Tell Wendell I'll be back by quarter to four."

He kissed his mother, grabbed his backpack, and raced off on his bicycle.

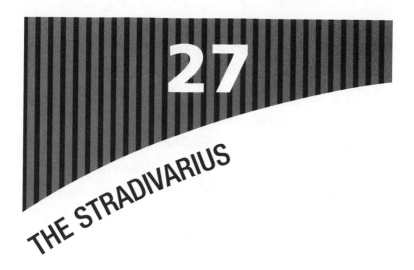

27

THE STRADIVARIUS

On the way to school the Hansen brothers tried to run Albert off the road. This time Albert didn't give way. This time he smiled at them and kept going, and after a while they drove on. He could see them looking back at him, like they couldn't figure out why he was still riding on the shoulder instead of barreling into a field of goats. He waved. They waved. He figured his relationship with the Hansen brothers had just improved.

He parked his bicycle in the rack outside the gym and joined the throng moving into the main building. He was five minutes early. On his way to class he spotted Mr. Grimes.

"You're never going to throw me out of school again," Albert said to the assistant principal.

Mr. Grimes looked down at Albert with a frown.

"You're not going to have to," Albert said. He hurried off as the warning bell rang.

He apologized to Mrs. Hissendale for saying her head looked like the planet Earth. He kept his mouth shut after that. He paid attention in every class. He decided that a couple of his teachers might actually be all right. When the last bell rang, he ran out of his classroom and down the hallway.

"Mr. Rosegarden!" Mr. Grimes called out. "No running."

"Yes, sir!" Albert yelled back. He downshifted to the pace of a racewalker.

When he reached the door he started running again. He grabbed his bicycle. He flew like the wind through town and up the dirt road.

Hollywood came boing-boinging out of the trailer to greet him. The camper bus was gone.

"Where's Wendell?" Albert yelled.

Elly was in the kitchen. "He said he was going grocery shopping."

"When will he be back?"

"I don't think he's coming back," she said.

"You told him to go, didn't you? It's your fault he's gone."

"I didn't tell him anything," she said.

"He was going to stay," Albert yelled. "He wanted to stay. You should have given him a chance."

"He got up. We had coffee. He said he wanted to contribute by stocking up on food. He left."

"Maybe he had an accident," Albert said. "Maybe he had another episode."

"What are you talking about? What kind of episode?"

"He was sick in Seattle. They took him to the hospital. He said he was all right and we left."

"If he was sick he didn't show it," Elly said. "He never tells the truth, Albert."

"We have to look for him."

"I drove around town twice," she said. "I went to the grocery store. Nobody there saw him. He's gone. That's what he does."

Albert went to his room and shut the door. For a moment he thought he'd go crazy. Wendell wasn't coming back. Everything he'd gained, he'd lost. He wanted to yell and scream and punch the wall. Then he saw it.

The Stradivarius was sitting on his bed. At least it looked like the Stradivarius. But it couldn't be. He'd given the Stradivarius to Reo Bascom. The key was attached to the handle with a piece of string. Albert unfastened it and unlocked the case. Inside was fifty thousand dollars and a letter. The letter was typed. Albert knew right away that Wendell had written it on Little Royal the night they'd stayed over at Big Royal's.

"Dear Albert," the letter read, "I didn't leave because of you or your mother. I never had more reason to stay somewhere than here, but it's not in me. I've lived my life on the move and I can't stop now. So I'm off to see the rest of the country's natural wonders. The violin case is the one I started out with. Reo Bascom has a phony. The money is for college or whatever you decide. What you tell your mother is up to you. I know you can handle it, Albert. You can handle anything. Love, Wendell."

He read the letter a second time. He felt a lump in his throat. He knew he'd never see his grandfather again. He closed the violin case and brought it to the kitchen and set it on the table in front of Elly.

"Where'd you get that?" she asked, setting Hollywood on the floor.

"Wendell left it," Albert said.

"It looks like the Stradivarius."

"It is," he said.

"You said he left it in Seattle."

"I thought he did," Albert said. "You should open it."

She looked at the case like it might bite her.

"It's unlocked," Albert said.

She lifted the lid and stared at the contents.

"It's fifty thousand dollars," Albert said. He heard his mother's sharp intake of breath.

"We can't keep this," she said. "Not the way he made it."

"I have something to tell you," Albert said. "Maybe after that you'll change your mind."

When he finished the story of Reo Bascom and the con and all the people involved and his part in it, she was quiet for a long time. Then she closed the case and said she'd think about it.

"We'll talk in the morning," she said. "We'll figure out what to do together."

He watched his mother drive off to work, then locked the case and hid it under his bed. He let Hollywood out and sat on the steps. The dog sat next to him. He thought about his grandfather and how the few days they'd had together weren't enough. Not nearly enough. He heard his grandfather's voice inside his head.

"I'll carry a letter that says to contact you when I kick the bucket," Wendell whispered. "You'll take care of things."

"I will," Albert said. "But I hope it's not for a long time."